There's

SOMETHING

Under the
Bed-Time Stories

Vol. 9 of Indian Creek Anthology Series

There's Something Under the Bed-Time Stories
Volume 9 of the Indian Creek Anthology Series

Published by Southern Indiana Writers, 2200 Reno Ave., New Albany, IN, 47150
or   2868 Alonzo Smith Rd., Georgetown, IN 47122

Book designed by T. Lee Harris

ISSN 1085-357X
ISBN 978-0-578-03570-3

Cover Art and design by T. Lee Harris
Back cover copy by Dirk Griffin

First Edition 2002
Second Edition 2009

Contents

Apex
by
Jeannine Baumgartle

The screen door rebounded to a close, and Helen knew her four-year-old daughter had gone outside to play. The sunshine coming through the hallway *was* magnetic, more than a child could resist, about as much as a grown-up could resist, truth be told.

A quick check at the window told her Wren was in her swing, pulling on the rope, kicking her way back and up. It was not a bad place to be. The hills rose and fell with each push, morning light overflowing the V-shaped horizon, coloring each of the hills in turn. The hesitation at the apex of the swing, the height of the view, was an epiphany strained toward again and again. Helen knew this because that's how it was for her when she was little, and the rapt attention her daughter paid to the art brought back all the memories. Wren was a child of nature, no doubt about it. There would be rocks in her pockets, leaves and twigs in her hair, and more than one bouquet of uprooted wildflowers she'd have to find a vase for. And that would be the apex of Helen's morning, or afternoon, receiving those flowers and the hugs that accompanied them.

She invented a sigh and gave up watching. The dishes and laundry ought to be started, the dog fed, the clutter straightened from the evening before. The newspaper she saved for making paper-doll chains and trees and boat-hats.

Her work took time, but Wren was okay, and called back whenever she checked on her. So far she'd been behind the barn, digging; in the catalpa tree, petting the cat; and in the dusty driveway, making footprints.

Such a nice bedroom for a child, she thought as she put folded clothes in the drawers of Wren's dresser. The room was blue, the color of the sky, the old white bookcase full and running over with books. Helen had made the curtains out of muslin, and she and Wren had traced around puzzle pieces with indelible markers in red, yellow, blue and green, to make shapes on them. Trucks and planes and bottles and ducks and rabbits and stars all fluttered softly in the breeze from the open window. They seemed today to have something clinging to them.

She lifted a corner of the fabric, and quickly let it drop. Worms, tiny little worms were making their way up the folds. They were climbing the wall, as well. The floor was worse, especially near the bed. She lifted the dust ruffle and looked underneath.

Snails, white slimy snails, had set sail from the corner, from a nest of acorns and blue-gray shells. The acorns must have hatched in the warm corner like incubated eggs. The bugs were all in the sheets and bedding, and had probably invaded the drawers as well. Grimacing, she gingerly stripped the linens from the bed and carried the buggy mess outside. The curtains would have to come down, the rug inspected for squashed bodies. All the books would have to be gone through and probably the closet cleaned out. She was in the hallway, getting a dust-pan when Wren came in.

"Watchyou doing?" her daughter wanted to know, and she told her about a very bad mess in the bedroom that she could help clean up. Wren even carried the broom. When Helen pulled the bed away from the wall, however, and tried to sweep, Wren intervened immediately.

"They're my friends," she protested, hot and bothered in an instant, and there was no reasoning with her, no easy way to explain.

Standing there, broom in hand, Helen considered how much of nature she could accept. You couldn't just take the rainbows and waterfalls and caves and gardens and forests, and deny the existence of whatever didn't appeal to you, like the tornados and hurricanes and earthquakes and floods. Even with a delightful force of nature like a baby, you had to accept the diapers and spitting-up and crying. It was all one piece. Her daughter knew nature, and accepted it all at face-value.

Helen found a cardboard-box lid, and under Wren's careful scrutiny, slid a paper under the nest of acorns and shells and transferred them to the lid. When they had rounded up all visible "guests," she sent Wren out to the barn with them, to introduce them to their new home. While she was gone, Helen cleaned and swept like crazy.

Bunk

by
Marian Allen

You always hear about identical twins who have the same characters—know each other's thoughts—feel each other's pain. It never was that way with my brother and me. If he had felt my pain, he wouldn't have smiled so much. If I had known his thoughts, I'd have dodged some pain, since he caused most of it.

And *he* was supposed to be "the good one." He was the one with the ready grin, open and easy with the grown-ups, undetectably manipulative with the other kids. I was the sullen one; silent, solitary, plain-spoken, blank-faced or scowling, humorless and dull.

"Angel Boy and Devil Boy," our Aunt Nan called us.

"Look at Andrew," she would say, pointing to my brother. "Look at that smile. He's so sweet, butter wouldn't melt in his mouth." She'd hold out an arm and he would come to her for a hug. He'd peck her cheek, then step behind her and make a face.

"And look at Edward," she'd say in a gruffer tone, flapping a hand in my direction. "Pure evil," she'd say, drawing it out with relish. "Pyooorr eeevuhhhl."

Somebody would push me within reach, and she'd wrap me in an arm like the tentacle of a giant squid and pull me close. She'd hold me there, a glowering captive, while she talked with Mom and Dad. Eventually, she would give me a hug and say, "I just love to torment him, 'cause he's so eevuhl." Then she'd crow with laughter and slap her leg. "Run along, you old savage."

Three or four times a year, Drew gets drunk and gives me a call. It's usually in the wee hours, but Drew went west while I went east, and the wee hours are bigger where I am. I'm usually up when he calls, sometimes dressed and drinking coffee, but I curse and mumble and pretend I'm half asleep. It takes so little to make him happy.

He used to call from home but since he got a cell phone I've had calls from parties and bars. I prefer those, actually, because he gets distracted during those, or lured away by something of more immediate interest.

"I just want you to understand," he says, without even saying hello, continuing a conversation he had begun in his head before he dialed. "It's important for you to understand."

Drew has had a series of therapists since he turned thirty and added "go into therapy" to his status symbol scavenger hunt. Whatever else he tells them, he apparently always includes his hatred of me, because his latest insight is the catalyst for these coast-to-coast heart-to-hearts.

"I never *did* like you," he'll say. "Never *did*. You want to know why?"

I've tried smart-ass answers: "Because I look like you?" "Because Mom always liked me best?" "How long did Cain hate his brother? — As long as he was Abel." They don't deflect him. Now I just say, "Why?"

I've made a list. My twin brother has always hated me because:

1.) There should only have been one of us. I usurped half of what rightfully should have been his. His vivid, outgoing personality is proof that he is the dominant twin and should have been the only one. I should have been absorbed by him during the early stages of gestation, but my perversity caused me to resist the natural process.

2.) I am not a real person, I am Drew's Shadow Self. He is unable to defend himself against his competitors at work because I contain his strength and guile.

3.) Nobody liked me, and it traumatized him to see somebody who looked so much like himself being so thoroughly disliked. Of course, I deserved it.

4.) I put him into analysis by speaking one word on September 30, 1959.

Personally, I don't believe he hates me now or hated me then. I think he uses hatred as a justification for his being a creep. But that's just my own unvarnished opinion, unsanctioned by the nod of a highly-paid professional.

"I'm telling Mom what you said about her!" This was Drew, the day we turned nine.

"Liar! I didn't say anything about Mom!"

Two boys, crammed into a room intended for one, do tend to get on one another's nerves.

"Did too!"

"Did not!"

"Did too!"

Technically, I *had* said something about Mom. It's a regrettable feature of our language that all the really good insults against males reflect on the morals of their mothers.

"I'm telling!"

And he did.

The party sounded great. I could hear it from up in our room. I was supposed to be thinking about what I'd said.

Mom came up to talk to me not long after the guests arrived. I could tell she was looking for an excuse to let me go, but I couldn't help her.

"There are better ways of expressing ourselves besides calling names, aren't there?" she asked.

"Yes, ma'am."

"What could you do instead?"

"Knock his block off."

Nope—wrong—bad answer. No party for me.

I was glaring out the window, hoping everyone would get stomach-aches, when a pick-up truck pulled up in front of our house.

Aunt Nan popped out of the passenger seat, followed by her son, Cousin Rob. Her husband, Uncle Ray, got out of the driver's side. Rob and Uncle Ray were built just like Aunt Nan only more so: tall and thin, with arms and legs like pipe-cleaners.

Strong, though. When Uncle Ray let down the back of the pick-up and tugged at the gift-wrapped rectangle in the back and Aunt Nan shrieked that he was tearing the paper, he climbed into the truck bed and hefted the slab in his arms. Rob stood on the street and Uncle Ray passed one end of the huge package to him then jumped down. They carried it between them like a stretcher, silver bow face-upward.

Just before she passed out of my line of vision, Aunt Nan looked up and our gazes locked. She hunched her head down into her shoulders and shook a finger at me. I heard her come in downstairs shouting,

"What's he done now? Can't even come to his own birthday party!"

Drew and I were close until some time after we turned four. I can remember our playing together, wanting to wear matching outfits—we even had a private language. We only used it when other people were around, never when we were alone. I still remember a few words: *orlo* meant *truck* or *car*, *teel* meant *snack*, *nayda* meant *no*. I still use *nayda*. Everybody at the office has picked up on it. Jeff, my cubicle mate, tells me it's the only word of Bolivian he knows....

When we were four, Mom went back to work part-time and Drew and I went to pre-school. That was when Drew started telling me he hated me. After he and his new friends knocked me down and made me eat grass, I started hating him back.

It always showed on me, though, and it never showed on him. What was "good-natured teasing" when he did it was "mean and nasty" from me. Complaints that got sympathy for him got me the order to stop whining. So I stopped looking for support and learned to endure. By the time I was six, I learned this.

It was some time during first grade (in different classes, by Drew's request) that he started with the bed.

"Better check under your bed, Eddy," he said, snuggling into his own.

"What do you mean? Why?"

"Just better. You never know."

My heart thumped. *You never know what?* I was afraid not to know, but I was afraid to ask. He had friends—maybe they told him something, something my friends would have told me, if I'd had any. Maybe Mom and Dad didn't tell me because they didn't want me to be scared of something they couldn't protect me from. Maybe Drew didn't really hate me, and he wanted to warn me. *He's just trying to scare me.* But maybe he wasn't....

Warily, I slid out of bed and checked.

"There isn't anything under there."

"Nothing you can *see*."

Chill. Fear. Dread.

"What do you mean?"

"Nothing. I'm just playing." He snapped out the light, leaving me on my knees in the dark.

I never snuck downstairs to watch The Twilight Zone through the banisters ever again.

Drew did, though. I would lie awake, gripping the edge of the covers. Drew would come up, whisper, "Better check under your bed," and slide between his sheets. Then he would tell me all about the show I had been too afraid to watch, hissing its terrors through the shadows.

I would stare into the gloom as long as I could, preferring terror to nightmare. Scared to get up in the night, I would wet the bed.

"Drew has never been a minute's trouble," Mom and Dad would say, tousling his hair. "But poor Eddy...." And I'd get a hug that felt like a consolation prize—the gift they give the loser.

It never occurred to me that anything under my bed might be under Drew's bed, too. It seemed all too likely that my side of the room would be infested, and mine alone. Even when I was old enough to know nothing was under my bed, I lay awake with all the gibbering specters that crowd a young boy's merry, carefree life elbowing for room beneath me.

When I went to camp (church camp, while Drew went to Scouts), I didn't have "accidents," although everybody knew my parents had warned about it on my intake form. When Drew spent the night with a friend, or when I did, I stayed dry. This was discussed openly at family gatherings.

Aunt Nan bumped open the door, which never would latch, and kicked it closed behind her. She carried a bowl with a spoon in it in one hand and a glass of fizzy red liquid in the other.

"Here." She plonked bowl and glass down on the lamp table between the twin beds. "Cake and ice cream and soda pop. Nobody's ever going to say any nephew of mine missed his birthday treats when I was around to do anything about it. Sit down and eat."

Mom would have saved me some, but it wouldn't have been the same after the party was over. It would have been like another punishment, another booby prize.

I sat on my bed and ate.

Aunt Nan sat on Drew's cowboy blanket. "That your bed?"

I nodded, mouth full.

"Why don't you put your feet on the floor?"

My feet, as usual, were up—heels on the bed frame, toes curled tight.

I didn't answer.

"Be that way, then," Aunt Nan said. She sat there, arms crossed, legs crossed, right foot bouncing, watching me. "Guess what we got you," she said at last. "It's for both of you."

"I don't know." I hated guessing games, and the thought of having to share a present with Drew took all the joy out of it.

"Guess."

"I can't."

"It's something you already have, but different."

"I don't know."

She patted the covers on either side of her.

I gave it a shot: "New blankets. With rocket ships on them."

She shook her head.

"I give up."

"You give up too easy. Everybody thinks Drew beats you at everything, but he doesn't. You give up."

I stopped eating and stared at her. Somebody knew. Somebody else knew.

"Well, are you going to guess again?"

"No."

"Oh, you're no fun! All right, I'll tell you. Bunk beds. Now what do you think of that?"

Bunk beds. *Bunk beds!* One bed on the floor, and one up in the air. One up in the air, away from the floor!

"You two will have to fight it out to see who gets which bunk," Aunt Nan said. "Knowing you, evil as you are, you'll probably say you want the opposite from the one you do want, just to be contrary."

Drew burst in. "Party's over—Guess what we got? Bunk beds!"

"I want the bottom," I said.

"Too late! I already got dibs, and *I* want the bottom."

Aunt Nan slapped her legs and laughed.

By the time we outgrew the bunks, Billy and Carol had been born, and we had moved to a house where we each had a tiny room of our own. The night of our ninth birthday Drew and I slept side-by-side for the last time.

"Better check under your bed, Eddy," Drew said, and snapped off the light.

It wasn't there. The frozen lance in my belly, the icicle in my heart—it wasn't there. There was nothing under my bed.

I grinned in the darkness. I knew by the feel of it on my face what it looked like: it was the grin of a prisoner set free after one too many days. It didn't feel pretty.

Mom read the directions and Dad put up the bunks—The four corner posts, the head and foot boards, the side pieces, all bolted together; the boards the mattresses would lie on that the instructions called "slats," seven slats for the bottom, seven slats for the top. Springs, half the thickness of the ones on our old beds, and mattresses, also half-thick. The beds were a little lumpy, and creaked and *poinged* when we moved, but we were at the age where a certain amount of discomfort held a sort of glamour.

Some bunk beds came with ladders, but this was a "real" one that a boy had to climb and haul himself into. It was great.

No *Better check under your bed* from Drew, but he wasn't a one-trick pony. I was almost asleep when the mattress beneath the small of my back heaved.

"Cut it out, Drew!"

"I'm not doing anything."

Heave.

"Keep it up," I said. "Knock one of the slats out, wise guy. See how you like a lump on the head."

"I'm not going to knock one of the slats out, crybaby."

Heave.

Every time the mattress bucked I felt like I was flying over the edge into empty air. I clenched my teeth and endured.

"You better not wet the bed up there," my brother said. "If you do, you'll be sorry. And I don't just mean from Mom." *Heave.* "I'm your worst nightmare."

That's when I said it.

"*Nayda.*"

No heave. Drew's voice: "What?"

"*Nayda.*"

I wondered if he remembered. He did. "That's just for when people are around."

I didn't answer.

"There's nobody here but us," he said.

"*Nayda.*"

"Cut it out! There's nobody in here!"

"*Nayda.*"

"Oh, what, like there's somebody under *my* bed?" Loudly sarcastic.

"*Nayda.*"

"Not in the closet, either! There isn't anybody in the closet!"

"*Nayda.*"

"Cut it out, Eddy! I mean it!"

"*Nayda,*" I whispered.

"I'm telling Mom!"

But what could he tell her? That I said there wasn't anyone in the room with us?

He was weeping with frustration and denial by the time Dad thundered in to tell us to pipe down and get to sleep. By the end of the week, he dreaded bed time as much as I ever had.

Come to think of it, maybe there's a little truth to that twins-sharing-character stuff after all.

Aunt Nan is still my favorite relative. If it hadn't been for her, I might never have learned that sometimes the thing beneath the bed is the boy in the upper bunk.

Don't Look Under the Bed
by
Elizabeth J. Gross

When bedtime comes, and Mama comes to tuck me in,
She kisses me on the head, turns off the light, and then,
I hear the closet open and **IT** comes in my room again.
The same as it did last night and also the night before,
It squishes, grates and slithers across the bedroom floor.

It crawls under my bed, and I hear it scrape the springs,
Then, it's *there!*—nestling among my things.
I don't know what it says—it tells me whisperings.
And, I'm so very much afraid, listening to this part,
Trembling, trembling, here lying in the dark.

Good night, it clearly says, as it crawls out again.
It squishes, grates and slithers on the floor, and then,
Goes back to the closet where it's always been.

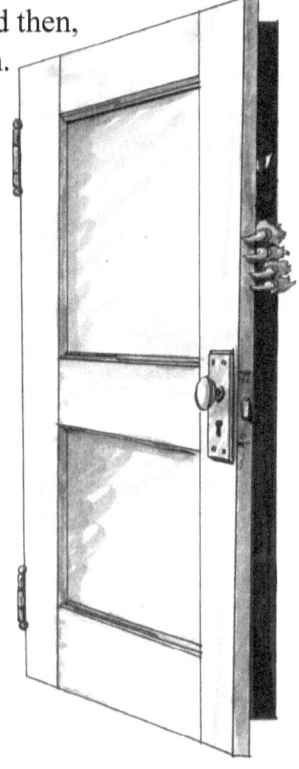

Day of the Dead

by

Mary Gehant-Lagunez

Mai Guthrie woke up in the sunny hotel room, stretched and reveled in a very satisfied feeling. Everything was going according to her well-thought-out plan, and soon she would be starting home to begin the life she wanted.

It had all been so simple, once she had made up her mind to it. But then, good planning had always been one of her best talents. In fact, that had been the reason why Winslow Guthrie had picked little Maybella Johnson out of the steno pool when he reached a position which required a private secretary. As he rose through the executive ranks, so had she, first becoming executive secretary, and then his administrative assistant. And she'd dropped that damned lower-class "Maybella" for the more sophisticated Mai.

Not that the new name had helped much, after Guthrie's first wife died and his so-helpful, sympathetic assistant became the new Mrs. Guthrie. His friends were also his business associates, so their wives continued to regard Mai as just "a little clerical girl," definitely not their social equal. They had tolerated her because of Guthrie, not quite insulting her but definitely keeping her at a cool distance. After his retirement, they became even cattier. Well, *that* won't matter any more.

She'd persuaded Guthrie to take a long vacation trip after his retirement. (Even after 12 years of marriage, she still thought of him as Guthrie, the same term she'd used at the office.) They had picked Cuernavaca, Mexico, as their destination. Guthrie had enjoyed his two-month stay there, studying Spanish when the company was considering opening a new plant in South America. He'd even made a few friends, and continued a lukewarm correspondence with one or two of them.

Mai hadn't kept up with anyone from home, or from the office, either. Unless she counted Sue Ellen, who'd been *her* junior, when Mai was still working. Sue Ellen became Guthrie's administrative aide when Mai married Guthrie and quit her job. Inevitably, she'd had to chat briefly with Sue Ellen whenever she'd called Guthrie at the office. And whenever Guthrie (and she) took a business trip, Sue Ellen had always asked Mai to send her a postcard from out of town. ("I can't travel now because Mom's not really well, and I do like getting postcards.") It hadn't been much to ask, or for Mai to do.

All through this trip, Mai had sent cards with pictures of the places along the way. She'd kept copies of the cards for herself, too, to be sure that she didn't keep saying the same things. She'd probably destroy those before she returned home.

She'd looked through those cards just the night before. On the way down, they told about Mai and Guthrie going through Graceland, pictures from Birmingham and the French Quarter, one of the Alamo, another from Laredo, just before they crossed the border. Now, during the past weeks in Cuernavaca, there was a change in the messages:

"Oct. 14. Guthrie called one of his old Mex. friends last night. There's to be some sort of a party tonight—I'm staying in the hotel. Can't speak Spanish, so why go?"

"Oct. 15. Guthrie met an old girlfriend at the party. She's a widow now, with a raft of kids, he says. She's probably fat and dressed in frumpy black, like so many of the women I see here."

"Oct. 17. Dragged to lunch with Guthrie and his old flame. I don't like her. She must spend a fortune on her clothes. Speaks English, but kept talking Spanish to Guthrie."

"Oct. 22. Guthrie has been playing golf mornings with Isabella (that's the bitch's name) at some fancy club—Taba-something. Yesterday and today, they stayed for lunch, too. ???"

"Oct. 26. Isabella insisted Guthrie and I have dinner at her house last night. Large, two maids, she's got money. Other people there, Guthrie spent all his time with her. I don't like it."

Mai bathed and dressed at a leisurely pace and headed down for breakfast. She was surprised to see a display with bouquets of large, brilliantly orange flowers near the front desk—they'd never had that, before.

"Buenos dias, Señora." The desk clerk's smile was a cheerful greeting.

As she came closer, she noticed portraits of an elderly couple between the two vases of flowers. Something about their clothes made

Mai think the pictures were taken some time ago. And also—candles, some fruit, a glass of something (tequila?) and little white things...*skulls.* Skulls with flowers on them.

Mai shuddered.

"What's that, with the flowers?" she asked.

"The *ofrenda?* It's for *El Dia de Muertos,* the 'Day of the Dead,' *Señora.* Here, we remember our parents, our dear ones, who have died. The pictures, they are *Sr.* Martinez' father and mother. They built this hotel, so the señor puts their photos here, in the lobby."

"When did they die?" Mai repressed a shiver. She didn't like funerals or sickness. Let the dead lie quietly, that's what she thought. But if the old geezers had just died....

"Oh, 10 years—perhaps longer, I never knew them, and it is eight years that I have worked here."

That wasn't the answer Mai wanted. Sick, that's what it was. She suddenly didn't have quite as much appetite as she had had earlier.

A good walk after breakfast would help her mood, Mai thought. After scanning through *The News,* the English-language paper the hotel handed out to guests, she set out. There were small shops along the street and window-shopping was one thing Mai liked to do.

She stepped along as briskly as she could, considering the narrow, somewhat broken sidewalk and the number of other pedestrians. A jeweler's, a place offering Internet access at five pesos an hour, a dress shop, small laundry, then a place selling those ruffly paper things— 'peen ... whatever' they call them. A clown, Mickey Mouse, a horse or mule or something...and two skeletons.

Mai shivered. What's this with dead things? She returned to the hotel and spent most of the day by the pool. The sun didn't seem as warm as it was a few days ago. That evening, she wrote another card to Sue Ellen:

"Oct. 29. Guthrie and the bitch are out, again. I bet something's going on. I'd like to head home, but he says why go back to cold weather? Because I want to leave here, that's why. He doesn't listen."

The next morning, after breakfast, Mai headed back to the Internet shop and pulled up *The Courier-Journal.* She wasn't much interested, but it passed the time. No news which caught her eye.

Maybe it was time to go on to the next step in the plan. She let a

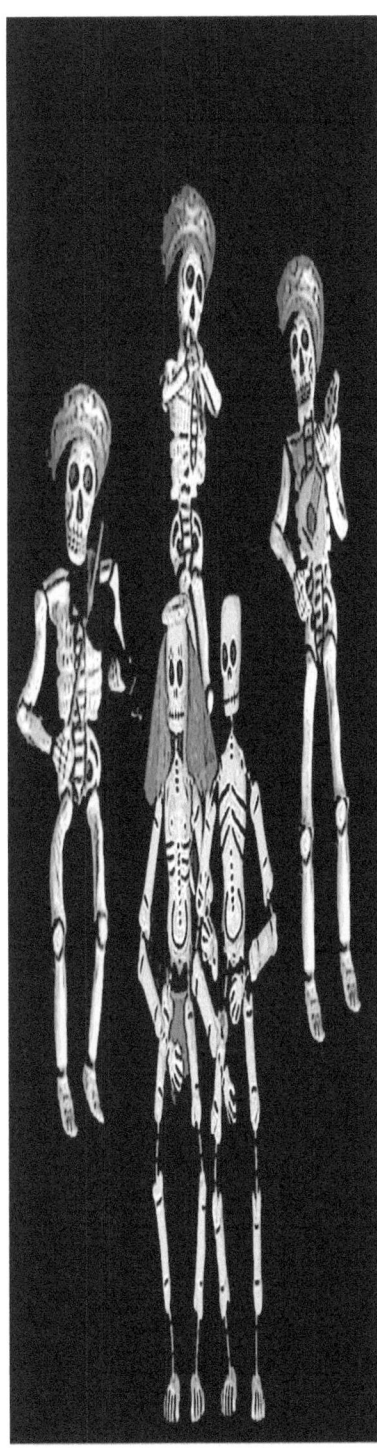

couple of days pass, then wrote a real letter to Sue Ellen:

"Oct. 31…can't write this on a card and have to spill to someone. Guthrie's left me…that Mexican bitch with all the money…he says I can have everything, but what good is that without a husband to help spend it?…I'm leaving here as soon as I can…. Long drive back all alone…Fine thing, I give my whole life for that SOB and he does this."

She mailed the letter the next morning, when she went out to Plaza Cuernavaca and Sanborn's. God, she was tired of that menu, but it was real American food. Either a club sandwich, a chef's salad or hamburger, usually. Today she celebrated with filet mignon, fries and lettuce and tomato.

After leaving the restaurant, Mai turned towards the book section of Sanborn's, through the bakery. And there, on the first shelf, were rounded loaves of bread with crosses baked onto the top and sides.. Instinctively, she looked the other way, towards the cash register counter. In back, the cakes—large cakes, right at eye level. A coffin with four candles on one, another with a skeleton. She hurried past the candy counter—which featured chocolate creams with skulls.

Mai almost ran out of the store. She didn't sleep well that night.

The following morning, she again took a walk after breakfast, but this time, most of the little shops were closed, including the Internet one. She felt a little uneasy as she returned to her hotel, but couldn't say why. All those death things around, and the shutters on the stores. That had to be it.

She asked the hotel clerk why the shops were shut up. "It's a holiday, *Señora, El Dia de Muertos,* they will open tomorrow. Can we get you something?"

Mai inquired, and found out that she could get the Net at the hotel. After surfing for a bit, she again pulled up the *Courier.* The photo and story jumped out at her:

"The body found in Harrods Creek two days ago has been positively identified as that of Winslow Guthrie, retired businessman who was presumed to be on a vacation trip with his wife....Guthrie's former secretary, Sue Ellen Dixon, gave Jefferson County Police postcards she had received from Mrs. Guthrie...

"The police are instituting a search for Mrs. Guthrie, who is believed to be in Cuernavaca, Mexico. They are contacting the Mexican authorities...."

The story went on to say that a fisherman had snagged his hook on the body, and the Kroger Plus card in the jacket had led to the identification.

A grocery card, in the pocket, when he always carried his cards in his wallet. Damn. It was such a good scheme, and she'd been so careful. A double dose of sleeping pills in Guthrie's bedtime cocoa, suffocating him with a pillow and then an early morning start with Guthrie "sleeping"—oh, yeah—in the back seat. Rolling him into the creek at an out-of-the-way spot, with the body weighted down. God damn that guy who was fishing.

Mai had really looked forward to having all of Guthrie's money, without Guthrie himself. But right now, she needed to make some new plans. Fast.

Gone

by

Bonnie L. Abraham

The battered green Chevy coughed and sputtered and died. Paul sighed and tried to start it again. All it would do was make a weak, grinding sound.

"Oh, great," groaned his sister, Rita. "Here we are out here in no-where-land and you've run out of gas!"

"Oh, shut up. It's not out of gas. I put in $5.00 worth before we left."

"I'll tell Mama you told me to shut up."

"Right now, Rita, I don't care," he growled. "Look. There's a house down there on the right. I think there's a light on in that front room. I'll go call for a tow."

"And leave me here by myself? I don't think so!"

"Well, you aren't going with me. You try and I won't drive you anywhere ever again."

"You will if Mama says," she retorted smugly.

"She won't say for me to if I tell her you won't mind me." Paul got out of the car, locked the door behind him and headed off down the hill to the old, two-story, white house. It looked to Rita like the setting of a Halloween movie. The house was badly in need of paint and the roof seemed to sag in the middle. Half the shutters at the upper windows were missing. She couldn't tell from this distance, but she would bet that much of the glass was broken out, too.

Rita checked her watch. "He's been gone a long time." The car had stalled beside a small stand of trees. The full moon cast the trees' shadows across the road and across the car. The wind caused the shadows to flicker and dance like flames. Rita nervously checked the locks on the doors and stared into the darkness under the trees, sure that she had seen something moving out of the corner of her eye, something besides shadows. But when she looked straight into the dark, she could see nothing. She checked her watch again. Had it only been ten minutes?

Finally she saw the door of the house open and Paul came out—

running. He ran to the car and she reached over and unlocked the door for him. He got in and slammed the door shut again, panting heavily.

"What happened in there? You look like you're scared to death!"

"I think you should get in the back seat - on the floor - in case they come out," gasped Paul between gulps of air.

"Who? —What's going on?"

"Rita, please—in the back, before they come out and see you!" It was the "please" that convinced her. Paul never said please.

"OK! OK! —I'm going! —But you better explain!" She half fell over into the back seat. —"OK, now...."

" I think they just killed somebody in there," hissed Paul.

"Yeh, right," responded Rita, her voice dripping with sarcasm. "This is another one of your pranks, isn't it? Well, gullible little sis isn't falling for it this time."

"No, really! Listen! While I was on the phone - with the garage, you know, I heard this scream—only it stopped right in the middle and the guy who pointed out the phone—gees, Sis, you should have seen this guy—anyway, he didn't seem surprised at all... I mean, he didn't even move! And there were candles everywhere, like a seance or something... really strange candles. They looked like they were floating."

"Maybe their electricity's off."

"I don't think so... no, it couldn't be, because they had one of those phones with the light... so you can see to dial in the dark, and it was lit. —Rita, do you know anything about witches?"

"Witches? Gees, Paul!"

"I think they're witches - having a meeting, like a coven. You should have seen this guy! He was dressed all in black and had a black cape, to the floor, and a hood pulled up so you couldn't get a look at his face —you should have seen him!" Paul's voice cracked with tension.

"Maybe they're having a Halloween party."

"Halloween's not 'til next week."

"So?"

"So, Stupid, they wouldn't be having a Halloween party until next week... and what about the scream? And the symbols?"

"What symbols?"

"The symbols on the floor, and on the walls... they were everywhere!"

"What kind of symbols?"

"I don't know. —Some kind of writing like Chinese or Arabic or something... you know... strange letters. I didn't recognize it."

"Well... it still might be just a party. A fun house maybe. Were you able to call the garage?"

"Yeh... and that's another thing. When I described where we were to Mr. Bunton, he wasn't too keen on the idea of sending someone out here this time of night. I asked for Mr. Ponds. I knew he'd come. But Bunton said he was busy." Mr. Ponds had moved in up the street from them just a couple of months earlier and worked at Bunton's Gas. "I'm not even sure he will tell him."

"Did he say he would... I mean after he knew where we were?"

"Yes, but I'm not sure I believe him." Paul jerked his head around toward the house. "Did you hear that?"

"Hear what?" squeaked Rita.

"You heard it. I can tell by your voice."

"You mean that 'screech-owl' sound?"

"That wasn't a screech-owl. That was another scream. And it came from the house. Rita, please get down. As far as they know, I'm alone. If something happens, you could still get away."

"Oh, Paul, really! Just what do you think is going to happen, any-way? —Looks like the party is breaking up."

"What? Oh, Lord, here they come! Get down! Pull that old blanket over you!"

"OK, but you have to tell me what's goin' on. And don't use 'Lord' like a curse, or I'll tell Mama."

"It wasn't a curse, it was a prayer... and I sure hope He heard! I think they're carrying a coffin," he whispered.

Rita's head popped up over the back seat. "Where?"

"Get DOWN!"

"I AM down! I'm looking between the seats," she argued, suiting her actions to her words. Peeking between the seats she saw the long, lozenge-shaped case with a circle of lights blinking in the center. The features of the two men carrying the case were hidden under drooping black hoods. "Gees, it does look like a coffin. But what are those lights?"

"I don't know. It looks kind of like one of those things they freeze people in for space travel in the movies. "

"Yeh, cryo-something. Move your arm. You're blocking my view!" Rita reached between the seats and poked him in the side.

"Stop it! If you don't behave, I'll tell Mother I'm not taking you with me any more," he threatened again.

"As if Mama will let you have the car again before you're thirty! It is after midnight, you know—on a school night. —Where did they go?"

"They went behind the house... and who said they knew a short-cut home and got us lost?"

"I did know a short cut—Mr. Ponds told me. Can I help it if I got it wrong? Anyway, who sat in front of Lucy's house and watched her get ready for bed and made us late to begin with? Besides, you were driving, so it's your responsibility not to listen to me when I tell you I know a short-cut. Whew! Where has this blanket been, anyway?"

"Here they come back. Stay down."

"Are they still carrying the cryo-thingy?"

"No... they must have set it down somewhere."

"Can I get up now? This blanket smells like the dog threw up on it."

"They're coming out again... with another one of those things. That must have been the second scream."

"Paul!"

"No, you can't get up yet!"

"I'll tell Mama about Lucy."

"Only if you live."

"Gees. I know this is another one of your stupid pranks... and if it is...."

"Jesus!"

"Paul!"

"Jesus! It's a space ship!"

"What?" Rita's head popped up over the back seat again.

They both watched as a fat, metallic, sausage-shaped object hovered beside the house, about four feet off the ground. Soft blue lights flashed in sequence, lengthwise around the object. The top of the "ship" reached just to the eaves of the house. As the two in the car watched, a hatch opened on the side and a set of open steps was lowered by someone or something inside. The men from the house, carrying their bur-

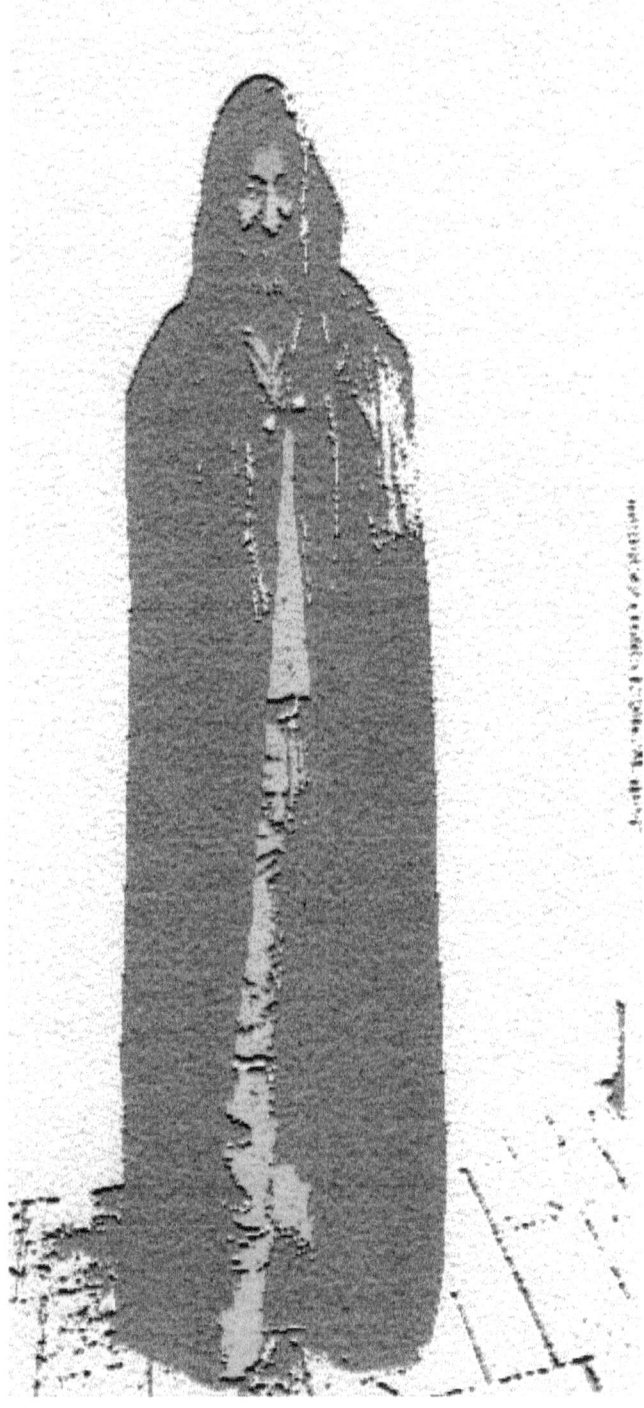

den between them, climbed up the steps and disappeared into the floating object, then reappeared empty-handed.

"It's not very big for a space ship," observed Paul.

"Maybe it's like a shuttle, you know, like the Galileo on the Enterprise."

Paul looked up through the windshield. "I don't see anything else," he croaked hopefully.

"It's probably too far up for us to see... or maybe it's one of those stars."

The two men disappeared behind the small ship and reappeared carrying the other case. They took it up the steps as well, then drew the steps up behind them. The door slid down with a bang that could be heard in the car.

"The lights are changing," said Paul. Sure enough, the lights no longer chased around the vehicle. They now glowed steadily and had gone from blue to red. The ship began to rise slowly. When it was above the roof of the house, it turned and began to move directly toward the car.

"I don't like the look of this," whispered Rita.

"Get DOWN!"

Rita ducked down behind the seat again, covering herself with the pungent blanket. Even under the blanket she could see the sudden light. "What's happening?"

There was no answer. Slowly, the light faded and Rita peeked out from under the blanket. She looked between the seats and saw no one. "Paul," she whispered, "Paul, where are you?" Still no answer. Slowly she raised up so that she could see over the seat. Paul was gone! "This is not funny, Paul!" She looked out the window. The shuttle was gone. The old house looked totally deserted. There was no sign of Paul anywhere. "Now what do I do?"

The minutes ticked by slowly. "I'm not getting out of the car," she said to herself. Then she noticed lights coming slowly down the road—headlights and a blinking gold light on top. Soon she was able to make out the shape of a tow truck. The truck pulled up opposite the car. She recognized the man who got out. It was Mr. Ponds.

He looked around carefully as he crossed the road to the car. "He doesn't appear too happy about being here," thought Rita. Tapping on

the window, he peered into the front seat. Rita saw the puzzled look on his face as he saw her in the back seat. He tapped again and pointed to the lock.

Rita's hand shook as she reached out and released the lock.

"Rita, you OK?" asked Mr. Ponds as he opened the door. "Where's your brother?"

"Gone," she said, her voice peaking hysterically. "He's gone."

"Went for help?"

Rita shook her head. "He's gone."

Mr. Ponds went around and raised the hood of the car. Rita watched as he jiggled a couple of wires, then removed a small black box and stuck it in his pants pocket. He came back around, got in the car and turned the key. The car started. "Loose wire," he said. "I'll drive you home and someone at the station can bring me back for the truck."

Rita waited a week. Then she couldn't stand it any longer. She had to go back to the house and look for Paul herself. She slipped out of the house, got out her bicycle and pedaled out into the country. It was dark by the time she reached the house. At the end of the drive, she got off the bike and laid it there on the grass.

The house was dark. Slowly, she walked down the drive to the door. She knocked, but there was no answer. She didn't know why she had expected anything else. As she turned to walk back to her bike, she looked up into the starlit sky. She was still looking up when she was surrounded by a blinding-bright light.

Mr. Ponds found the abandoned bicycle the next morning. He told the police that he had heard they were looking for the missing girl and, remembering the boy's disappearance the week before, had driven to the old house to check.

A week after Rita disappeared, Mr. Ponds drove out to the old house one more time. He parked the tow truck at the top of the hill and walked down to the house. When he knocked on the door, it was opened by a tall figure draped in a full-length, black cape. The creature had not pulled its hood up, and Mr. Ponds gasped involuntarily at the grotesque fish-like features.

"I've come for my payment."

"Enter," the creature responded, stepping away from the door.

Reluctantly, Ponds stepped inside, glancing around nervously. He cleared his throat, then reminded his host, "We agreed on $30,000.00 each." He was handed a brown rectangular case. The creature's webbed fingers left sticky, narrow trails on its surface. Ponds grabbed the case and turned to leave, but at the door, he stopped. "The first two..." he said without turning, "You said you would release them if I got you the kids."

"They have seen too much."

Ponds turned. "Take me too, then," he pleaded.

"You do not fit the specifications."

In a violent rage, Ponds leaped at the creature, swinging the case at its head.

The next morning, Ponds woke in the front seat of the truck, his head resting on a brown case. "Huh? What am I doing out here?" Noticing the case he opened the lid. It was full of money! "Whew," he whistled. "Where did this come from?" He closed the lid, then looked around. "Spooky looking old house," he whispered. "Wonder why I never noticed it before." Shivering, he started the truck and drove back to town.

Flower Cart
by
Jeannine Baumgartle

In a house
with no grace,
one day
a flower cart
four inches long,
red-flocked insides
around tiny bouquets,
a yellow center for
each miniature bloom;
this I remember,
even the window
I stood by
to take this in,
head full of color;
suddenly there
my grandmother's
papery little cackle
—not of delight,
at my weakness
for magenta.

Family Secrets

by

Glenda Mills

James Edward Collingsworth V eased his car along the flooded pavement of State Road 80. The windshield wipers on his Mercedes slapped helplessly against the wall of water cascading from the sky. Thunder boomed and lightning burned streaks in the clouds. James smiled. The tumultuous weather couldn't shake the his peace of mind. By tomorrow morning, the Collingsworth estate would no longer be his concern. The weight of four previous generations would lift from his shoulders with the stroke of a pen and a handshake to seal the deal.

His great-great-grandfather had left a sizeable fortune strictly for the maintenance of the family property, but the money was running out and James felt no particular attachment to the place. Lansford Developing, however, had fallen head-over-heels for the estate. They were looking for an authentic, pre-Civil War, southern plantation to turn into a private resort, bed-and-breakfast thing. Not only were the house and grounds in immaculate condition, but all traces of the institution of slavery had been erased by James' father. Lansford's patrons could enjoy the beauty without any reminders of the people on whose backs the place was literally built. Denial was definitely underrated. As long as Landsford brought him a nice, fat check, they could do whatever they wanted with the place—recreate Eden, if they thought they could find the blueprints.

The lights weren't flashing on the railroad crossing, but James stopped and looked anyway. He even braved the elements, opening his window for a moment and listening. A high school friend had died in a car-train accident, and it had left a permanent impression. There was no sign of a train tonight, so he crossed the tracks, traveled a couple more miles and turned onto a winding driveway. He couldn't see the trees that lined the gravel, but he knew they were there: magnolias, elms, standing sentry.

He pulled as close to the door as he could, grabbed his duffle bag and made a frantic dash for the front door. He slipped once on the steps, hitting his shin in the process, and despite all his efforts to hurry, was dripping water from his hair and clothes by the time he made it to the shelter of the porch. He rubbed his aching shin, wiped a drop of water from the end of his nose, and reached for his keys to unlock the front door. The keys weren't in his pocket.

"I'll be damned. I must have left them in the car." He decided to use the spare key, which was in the fake rock by the front door. If somebody was desperate enough to brave this God-forsaken weather to steal his car, so be it. That's what insurance was for.

There was a fire in the fireplace, supper waiting for him in the kitchen, and a freshly made bed, complete with turned-down sheets and a fresh snifter of brandy on the night stand. The house and grounds were kept as if the family still resided here. One phone call and the staff made sure everything was in order for his visit before they left for the evening. He'd scored with more girls in this house, especially the shallow ones who melted at the slightest hint of wealth and power. The house might be a financial albatross now, but he had to admit there were times when these walls had helped make his wildest fantasies come true.

The storm was still in full swing by the time James finished supper. He retired to his room, content with a good book and a full glass of brandy to lull him into a restful, early evening and drifted off after half a glass or so, the promise of a fortune of his own swimming lazily through his dreams.

The next thing he knew, he was awake—immediately awake—eyes wide open, sitting straight up in bed, trembling. He reached for the light on the bedside table, fumbled, and heard his brandy glass crash to the floor. Nothing happened when he turned the switch on the lamp. The power was out. Fumbling once again in the darkness, he opened the drawer of the bedside table, found a flashlight and turned it on.

As his eyes adjusted to the light, he heard a voice, a woman's voice, singing. "Who is that, no one else here, maybe it's the wind...." His confused mumbling soon congealed into a coherent thought. One of the maids must have returned for the night. He got out of bed, stepping carefully around the broken glass, only to stub his little toe on the bedpost. He limped out into the hallway, determined to give the insolent maid a piece of his mind.

After much stumbling and groping, he tracked the singing to a room at the end of the hall. For a moment, he was touched by the tenderness of the woman's voice, but then his toe throbbed with pain, and his irritation broke through again. He threw the door open, panning his small beam of light across the room.

"What in the ...?" Words broke off in his throat as the light came to rest on the figure of a young woman, rocking slowly in an old, wooden rocking chair. She was wearing a long dress and cradling something in her arms. The fragrant scent of lilac filled the room. The woman never acknowledged James' presence. She just kept singing, rocking gently in rhythm to her song, staring down at the sleeping infant in her arms. He didn't recognize her immediately, but it was obvious she wasn't a maid. He took a closer look. She had long, dark hair with soft waves of curl throughout. She was wearing a blue dress straight out of *Gone With the Wind*. There was a large sapphire and diamond pendant around her neck and a radiant glow on her face. Suddenly, it came to him. He had seen her before in a family portrait over the fireplace in the great room downstairs. Actually, what he remembered most was the necklace, that very large, very expensive necklace. She was one of his great-great-grandfather's daughters, which made her his whatever. If memory served him correctly, she had died early in her life from a fall which had broken her neck. There was never any mention of her marrying or bearing any children.

"Family secrets can be buried, but they can't be silenced." His grandfather had said that many times on various occasions, but he never elaborated with any specific examples or juicy details. Of course, a family with as much money and power as his was bound to have some skeletons in the closet. Bad choice of words considering the circumstances. What circumstances? James realized the woman had disappeared, if indeed she'd been there at all. Rational thought took over, bringing the whole ghostly sighting into focus. Take one stormy night, a dose of good old-fashioned guilt for selling out the family homestead, and a healthy glass of brandy and the result was one made-to-order spook. He'd wasted enough time on this foolishness. He turned toward the door, determined to get some sleep.

Before he could make good his escape, the door slammed shut. He could smell the mustiness of old fabric and see dust floating in his

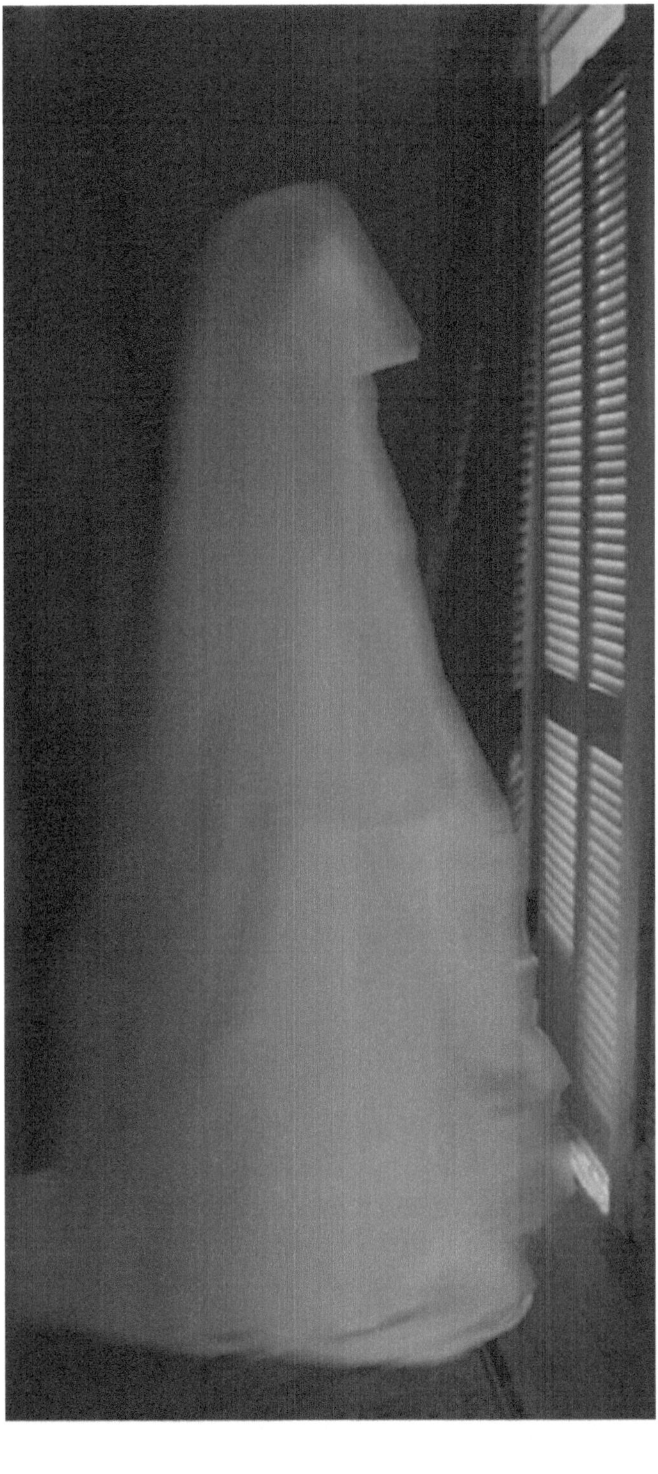

beam of light. He heard a baby crying and turned his flashlight in that direction. There was a cradle rocking violently. The infant's cries grew louder and louder. Suddenly, the figure of a man appeared, standing over the cradle. James knew the figure from paintings he'd seen around the house. It was his great-great-grandfather. The figure reached down with his hand into the cradle and the baby's cries were quickly muffled. Enough was enough. James reached around for the doorknob. The door was locked. He closed his eyes, hoping to convince himself this was some terrible nightmare, but when he opened them again, the figure was still there. The baby's cries had stopped completely. There was silence for a moment and then James Collingsworth I raised his ghostly face to the ceiling.

"Death to the bastard," he whispered and laughed, a chillingly gentle laugh that made his great-great-grandson's hair stand on end.

Just as quickly as he had appeared, the figure disappeared. The laughing stopped. James made his way on shaking, wobbly legs to the window. If he couldn't get out through the door, he'd settle for plan B. Landsford could send him the necessary papers and a check in the mail. He wasn't sure what was going on around him, and he still didn't buy the whole haunted house idea, but he had no intention of staying long enough to figure it out.

The window was stuck from years of disuse. He worked frantically, lifting and swearing, looking over his shoulder for any unwelcome visitors. He took a deep breath, ready to give the window one last manly heave before resorting to plan C, whatever that was, and bumped his elbow on a small, roll-top desk next to the window. An open book lying on the desk grabbed his attention, and despite his brush with the supernatural, he found himself straining in the dimness of his flashlight to read the faded writing on the dusty, yellowed page.

Father is furious and grows more sullen and terse each day. I fear my child is in danger for, even though the child is his grandson, Father seems unable to forgive the circumstances of his birth. Therefore, I have made a decision, one which is both painful and necessary. Tonight my love will come for me and our son. We will leave my father's house in secret and wed in a town away from here, where my father's name is not known. There we will start anew, free from the stares and whispers of the townspeople and the shame of our families. It is the only way we will ever be at peace.

For a moment, he forgot about ghosts and thought instead about the plight of this relative, a beautiful, wealthy, prominent woman who had abandoned it all for the sake of love; love of her child and love of a man. Had she made her escape? Did she and her lover ever have any more children? Did they find strangers willing to accept them?

Lilac once again filled the room, pulling him abruptly from his thoughts. This time he looked over his shoulder to see the same young woman he'd seen earlier hanging by her neck from a rope tied to a beam in the ceiling. Her scream mingled with his. James broke out the window glass with his flashlight, hurled himself out onto the lawn, his fall softened somewhat by mud and hedge, and ran for his car. He didn't look back until he'd cleared the driveway.

His hands were shaking so badly that he could hardly keep them on the steering wheel. He tried desperately to slow his breathing, clear his head, regain control. There were tears in his eyes. A couple of miles from the driveway, his car suddenly filled with lilac perfume, and he heard a soft, gentle voice singing tenderly in the seat beside him. His eyes left the road. He never saw the blinking red lights or the bright white light coming at him. He never heard the blaring sound of the train whistle. He saw a young woman cradling a baby in her arms. She smiled at him and then his world went black.

The Lover
By
Dirk Griffin

Polly Landry moved with poise among her many guests. Late August was not usually a time for affairs of this size, but she wanted to bask in the adoration of those who most envied her. She and her husband Jacob were acknowledged as the wealthiest family in Charleston, South Carolina, and in achieving that, among the wealthiest families in the youthful United States of the Americas. Having arrived at this long-sought position, she wanted the coming out party for her new home to be suitably grand. Grand was the only word to effectively describe Landry House. Situated on the most desired lot in Charleston, Landry House boasted views of the Ashley and Cooper Rivers as well as the Harbor. Because of its unique situation it featured three tiers of piazzas, which wrapped around three sides of the house and offered a magnificent overlook of the burgeoning aristocratic district on the southern peninsula. Jacob had indulged Polly's every whim in the construction of the house, allowing her to meet with the architects and designers, offer suggestions, and create a home to showcase their wealth. Her greatest excesses came in the interior details: many hand-painted murals, Italian marble mantles, meticulously detailed carvings, crystal from England, furniture from France and, in an impressive coup, the first house in Charleston with gas lighting. The plantation house was fine for family and time apart from the city but now, with the completion of Landry house, she could be in the limelight of Charleston's growing social scene, where she longed to be. On this lot overlooking the rivers, in the heart of Charleston's elite, she had gained all that she had ever hoped for in her marriage to Jacob.

1850 was an excellent year for Charleston. With the financial setbacks of the early 1840's and the Mexican war done, the social and economic prospects had begun to move upward at what seemed an ever-increasing rate. Charleston was now flowering, after years of dedicated work, into the "Queen City" of the South. It had become a city at last capable of standing shoulder to shoulder with New York, Boston, London, and Paris. Though there was no official aristocracy, one should never speak of that among the wealthy power brokers of this fairest of cities.

The Landrys had been married only six years, but in that time had produced four children and, between Polly's social activity and Jacob's business dealings, had risen to the top of the aristocratic food chain. Indeed, they were the couple all others watched and emulated. They had built a reputation for style and elegance that was envied and copied by their devoted following and derided by their few weak and envious detractors. Jacob, the eldest of his generation, had built, in spite of the economic problems that plagued the previous decade, on his father's holdings. He grew the agricultural business, left him by his father and based primarily on rice and potatoes, by adding tea fields—a new crop, but one well suited to the Carolinas. Immensely profitable and immediately popular, Carolina tea became the rage throughout Europe. He improved import and export operations by stocking his own warehouses and shops, and setting afloat his own fleet of ships, rather than hiring out. The addition of a company fleet to their assets, allowed him to better control and predict the prices that affected the family's fortunes. His acumen had moved the Landry family beyond all others. There was in fact not a close second, even among his younger brothers. Polly Landry came from one of the minor merchant families, but had proven herself equal to the task. Her desire for power and prestige played along with their wealth to create an almost mystical aura of nobility and privilege.

This coming out night of Landry House was a full-scale social assault. New music from Europe, pastries from France, beef prepared by the Landrys' latest acquisition: a chef hired away from a royal house in England. Here among her people, Polly was resplendent in her excess, and kind in her company. After a miraculously large meal served to nearly two hundred guests, the evening had reached the dance hour, and so, instruction in the latest dances from France and England, was underway. Some gathered on the beautiful piazzas, while others sat eating cakes and sipping tea in idle conversation. Polly moved strategically about the room reveling in the awe and worship of those in attendance. It was a moment of supreme triumph for her, nothing could possibly spoil this night – then she saw him.

He was Jonathan "Jack" Kinney just a boy when last she knew him, but she would know him anywhere. His eyes gave him away: they possessed a dark, faraway cast that drew her into him. She had heard that he died at sea, but she hadn't really believed it. She always thought that a simple lie told by her father to interest her in wealthier and more prominent men. Men such as Landry, who though twelve years her senior, had much to offer a young lady of ambition. Seeing Kinney now, in black trousers and frock coat, accented by a red waistcoat trimmed in white lilies, she could see how kind the years were to him. He was still handsomely built, only more so than when he was younger. One could make out the muscles of his powerful arms through the sleeves of his jacket. Without realizing it, she found herself stirred by the memory of her girlish love for him. What had she told him when they last stood on the dock? Was it that she would always be his and await his return? How silly and immature of her. It was a kindness her father had done for her. What could an impoverished sea dog such as Jack Kinney offer her? Despite his rugged good looks, he could never fill her need for the life of leisure and adoration that she enjoyed as the young Mrs. Jacob Landry. Finally she thought, *"You can dress our fine and handsome Mr. Kinney as well as any king, but he'll never have the wealth or offer the position that Jacob has given me."*

It was as she was having this final, dismissive thought that Kinney saw her from across the room. Their eyes met, and she felt herself ten years younger. This simple glance from a poor seaman turned her red and warm with excitement. *"Don't be ridiculous, Polly."* She told herself, *"He's just another man, certainly nowhere near the equal of your Jacob."* Time lost its meaning. She couldn't count the moments between her last thought and the warmth of his hand holding hers; she felt herself weaken as the soft, moist tenderness of his lips brushed against her hand.

"M' lady Landry," he spoke with a rich voice as deep as the ocean, "it has been so long."

"I'm sorry, good sir, I don't believe I've had the pleasure of making your acquaintance." She tried to play it off, as if he were just another in the line of men wishing to bask in her genteel company.

"Kinney," he began, "Captain Jonathan Kinney, though you may know me better as simply Jack." With the last he let a quick wink pass between them.

"I once knew a boy named Jack Kinney. Are you he, sir?"

"I see you do remember me, my dear." He paused to look about the room, taking in its wealth as if breathing in air. "And I see that you've done well for yourself in my absence."

"Well, my husband and I are blessed with prosperity and family; it is a good life I have here Captain Kinney."

"Jack, my dear, please call me Jack, let there not be any formality between us."

Polly looked closely at him. His crisp neatly trimmed beard was black against his richly tanned face. He had pulled his long dark hair into a tail and tied it with a red ribbon. And then there was his scent, his scent made it difficult for her to think clearly. How had he gotten here? He wasn't on the list, and surely he couldn't be with any of her guests, who would bring a simple sea captain to an affair of this magnitude? She stammered a reply that seemed rehearsed in its stiffness: "But, but sir, it wouldn't be right for a married lady of my stature to speak with such familiarity to a man other than her husband."

Jack continued, oblivious to her comment, "I could use a little air, Mrs. Landry. Could we perhaps step out on the piazza? I'm not used to such enclosed spaces."

She followed him, against her better judgement—possibly against her will. She was suddenly desperate, so desperate to hear him call her Polly once again. It was as if her mind had been taken from her. Here she had all she had ever thought she wanted, possessed of power and wealth. Yet, the appearance of this one man, whom she had loved dearly as a boy and for whose loss she had wept bitterly, with just a glance and few words had commanded more of her attention and touched more of her desire than anyone or anything had in years. As she moved entranced, toward the piazza off the ballroom, she stopped, as if remembering something. She saw Jack standing in the large double-arched doorway, his hand extended to her. She looked back: the music was unclear, and sounded distant. Was it now coming from somewhere down the street? How was that possible?

"Don't worry." It was Jack's deep and comforting voice. He was beside her again. "No one is watching, no one will see." With that she took his arm and exited to the piazza.

Once outside the house, Polly could feel the wetness of the air around her and the evening breeze off the ocean, heavy with the scent of salt. She looked up at Jack, and was swallowed whole by the experience.

"I'm a plain man, Polly, and I'll speak plainly to you. You are mine, you have promised yourself to me, and I mean to have you again."

This bald declaration cut through the spell and snapped her back to reality. "Captain Kinney, how dare you come into my house after all this time and challenge the authority of my husband in such a brazen manner? I knew you to be lowborn, but you possessed an air of refinement that led me to believe you had bettered yourself. I see now that you are simply a savage in finery, unaware of social graces."

"I spoke the plain truth to you, Polly. As you promised me the day I left you would be mine always, I will hold you to that promise, husband and children be damned."

That was enough. She had had all she wanted. No matter how attractive he might be, he would not lay waste to all she had put up with to reach this point in her life. She had money. She was envied, young, and beautiful. She would not throw it away on this churlish barbarian, no matter how she may have foolishly felt about him in her youth. "Captain Kinney," she pronounced, "that was ten years ago I was but a child, and I'll not have you hold me to those words." She snapped around in fury and began to move toward the ballroom, but Kinney caught her arm and swung her around, fixing his gaze on her, and again, she fell under his spell. Whatever it was, it was tangible. She could feel the depth and breadth of what he had endured to return pour into her. The pain, the suffering, and the overwhelming desire for her that swept away her manners and bid her think the unthinkable.

"Jack," she was startled to address him so personally. Some inner desire had flooded past the trappings of gentility, "Jack, how I've longed to say your name. But I can't be with you. I have what I want and fair though you are, I can't have both it and you."

"You can, Polly, you can," he insisted.

"I've Jacob—though not particularly attractive, he has provided for me—and the children to consider, I've a life here, power, position, all I could want and no matter how I loved you—how I might love you—now that I've had this, I can't give it up. Not for you, not for anything. This is my life, I will live it, more the sorrow to know that you live and I can never give my love to you again."

Kinney's eyes brightened as a smile moved across his face.

"Jack, you're not making sport with me are you? I couldn't bear to think you're making fun of me and my life."

Kinney's smile broke into a low and gentle laugh, "Polly, you don't think I'd be fool enough to come here empty of offerings for you. If one comes to worship a goddess he should come with offerings."

"Offerings? Whatever are you talking about Jack?"

Kinney turned to look out toward the harbor. In the distance over the ocean, summer lightning flashed in the rolling clouds. "I've had agents look into you and your life, I knew full well when I came here what had become of you, Polly. I'm a powerful man now. You may be a rich merchant-planter's wife, but you are still not royalty, are you?"

"What are you saying, Jack?" her voice trembled as the rumble of the lightning flash finally rolled through the harbor.

"I'm saying, my dear, that the years have been good to me as well, very good. I serve a king, and he has made me a Lord, granted me land, title, and servants. My holdings are nearly the size of both your Carolinas. I am the titled Lord of all I possess." At this point Kinney turned to Polly and looked directly in her eyes. The lightning flashed at sea again, as he continued, "I'll lay all that treasure at your feet if you will sit at my side as Lady of the Seven Hills of Inimicus."

Her mind raced, here was position, such as she had imagined, and a lover worthy of her charms – after all, she was considered by one and all the fairest flower of both Carolinas. Perhaps she did deserve more. But Jacob and the children, what of them?

"Yes, my love, yes, what of your family here?" His words were as smooth as silk on glass.

"How did you—" again, the thunder rolled over the harbor.

"I only asked what I knew you would be thinking. I have your answer, though you may not like it, Polly." His soft, sweet breath was warm as he continued, "They must die."

"Die?" She couldn't believe she had said the word, "How? Why?"

"Your husband must die, for while I can take you far from here, to lands covered in white lilies, full of wealthy, influential souls, and while I have armies at my command to keep you, he will not rest until he returns you to his side. We will never be free of him, unless he be dead."

"How, Jack? How do you know this?"

"I know, my love, because I would never rest until you were again by my side. Death itself could not stop me returning to you, but one as weak as your husband, maybe it could stay his hand."

Polly turned from him and as she did, she could feel his powerful arms pull about her waist. She fell back against him afraid she might collapse. She couldn't imagine, couldn't be a party to anything as ghastly as that. Then she asked the question for which she wanted, but didn't want an answer: "And the children?"

"You love them, not because they are his, but because they are yours, and a part of you. They will await you in eternity. But, if they remain here, alive, you will eventually desire to see them again; they will draw you out, and possibly from me. You must take their lives each one, kindly, gently, with as much grace as you possess, or you can never truly be mine again."

Polly Landry thought of her life, all that it meant to her, and then she sank more deeply into her lover's arms. He was no more the gentle youth she had loved beyond measure, but a self-assured, commanding man, brimming with power and he only wanted one thing in this entire world: her. She heard another roll of thunder move through the peninsula.

She turned again and looked deep into his eyes, searching herself for what held more meaning for her: The wealth and power she had built here with husband and children who were simply the trappings needed to sit in that state of social grace; then she considered being among royalty, holding vast lands and wealth. She looked at Jack and the youthful love she had felt flamed hot again for he was handsome, strong, and physically at one with the power he wielded. She didn't doubt him at all, and she found herself speaking words which a scant time before would never have crossed her lips, "Yes, yes, dear Jack, my dear, darling Jack, back from the dead," tears were filling her eyes in the confusion of desire, loss, and gain. "I'll go with you and be your lady. I will do anything you ask of me, even this terrible thing, if it will bring me back to you never to part."

"My ship leaves with the morning tide. You must be on it. This will be your only opportunity." Behind him the lightning flashed over the sea, "Here," he produced a small vial filled with a liquid red as garnet that glowed by the gas light on the piazza. "You must mix this with their final tea. When they sleep, they will not wake. Neither pain, nor suffering will fall upon them, save sleep eternal. After this, then come to me at my ship the Lady Grey, and we will be together forever."

"Yes, my love, forever." She grasped the vial. It seemed so hot that she thought it might burn her hand. "I can't believe you've come back for me with so much."

Kinney gently brushed a lock of hair from her cheek and softly pressed his lips upon her forehead. "Nothing could ever have kept me away. Soon, my love, soon together forever."

She pushed the vial into one of the pockets hidden among her dress folds and almost stumbled back into the ballroom. A rumble of thunder pressed through, under the uplifting melody of the dance, and she realized she couldn't remember how long she had been away from the party. What if someone had seen her? What if Jacob should ask after her or the dark captain she was with, what would she say? She invented stories and denials in preparation for what might come, but her mind slowly slipped into the business of being hostess and the rest of the evening passed in a haze of moments and people. Only two things stood out: she remembered clearly wishing Jacob dead and she seemed haunted by the deep dark eyes of Jack Kinney. When the party and the evening were done and the last guest had departed, she offered tea to Jacob and the children. Polly put them to bed, each with a kiss, but no sorrow or regret. Once they had fallen under the spell of the red liquid, she allowed herself a final look and was gone, through the brisk early morning air to the docks and the good ship, Lady Grey.

She was seen aboard and brought immediately to Jack. Before the first rays of sun had struck the deck of the ship she wondered what her friends in Charleston would say. Would they think the family poisoned and her stolen by some enemy? Gradually these thoughts faded as the ship sailed day after day. She felt release and bliss and eventually found she could no longer remember the faces of her family. It had become as if they never existed. She stayed day and night with her fair lover Jack, Lord of the Seven Hills of Inimicus.

A few weeks out, she first asked where his lands were. Jack obliged by showing her on the ship's maps their current location and where they lay in relation to them, they would, if fair weather stayed, be there in but a few more days.

That night she awoke to find Jack missing from their bed. Polly was suddenly gripped with fear; she could feel and hear a violent storm all about her as the ship rocked horribly. Quickly covering herself, she made her way to the deck. The waves rolled darkly, and the rain pelted down like shot. Lightning and thunder struck and roared in the same breath all around. Only the sight of Jack, silhouetted against the strikes of lightning, brought her any sense of peace. She made her way through the fierce winds to the ship's wheel, where he stood. She thought it odd that he seemed so calm amid the clamor of the wind and waves. She cried above the roiling storm, "Jack, where are the crew? What is happening?"

"They're about," he said flatly.

"Will things be all right?"

At this moment a great fork of lightning stabbed through the foredeck leaving a hole and a fire below.

Polly screamed, "Jack, what are we to do?"

Jack responded in a calm and clear voice, "There's nothing to be done, Polly." He released the wheel of the ship, and took Polly by the arm. Something about his touch restrained her terror and she looked into his eyes. "My dear Polly, I returned to Charleston two years and 223 days after I left you on that dock. All the time I sailed the sea, I could think of nothing but you. It had been a long and lonely voyage, but I had managed enough to start a business and prove myself worthy of your love. When I came to your door, your father told me you were gone and married to another, better off without me. I was so angry and naïve that I signed onto the first ship leaving port and swore I'd never set foot on land again." The storm raged about them, but they were undisturbed by it, Polly held in Jack's strong arms and transfixed by his eyes, he holding to the ship as it burned and broke apart beneath the storm. "I know now that you hadn't married yet, and I cursed myself for not asking outside your father's word on what he claimed. Within a year that ship went down with all its crew. I died with your name on my lips, begging for some power to bring you back to me."

Polly, held immobile by Jack's power yet aware of the chaos around her, felt the sting of the rain, and the stench of the smoke. Tears poured out of her as she thought of her life and what she had done. "No, Jack, no!" she sobbed. "What of your king, your lands, your title?"

"All true, for I serve my master even now as we go to join him in that land of darkness." Fire flashed in his eyes, was it a reflection of the burning ship or something more? Polly couldn't be sure and shuddered violently in his arms. "I'll show you the lilies of my fields, white as snow and plentiful, and our subjects, foolish, once-powerful souls who have given themselves up to him without knowing it. They serve me as they will serve you, my lady, in the deep kingdom of my liege."

Polly was wracked with sobs and her tears poured as forcefully as the rain. Unable to move or struggle, she finally felt the pull of the ocean as it surrounded them. At last the darkness of the deep sea enfolded her, for all eternity, in the arms of her lover.

The Shear Point
by
Bonnie L. Abraham

She spent her days
with needles and thread,
pins and scissors,
making gowns
for other women...
women who did not
appreciate her efforts.
"It's too tight in the waist,"
from the woman who insisted
her waist was 29 inches
and would not be measured.
"And the stripes make me look fat,"
though she had refused
all other choices.
"You could have warned me,"
she exclaimed.
"Not without calling you a fool,"
thought the seamstress
as she drove the shears
into the woman's heart,
(after having her remove the dress, of course.)

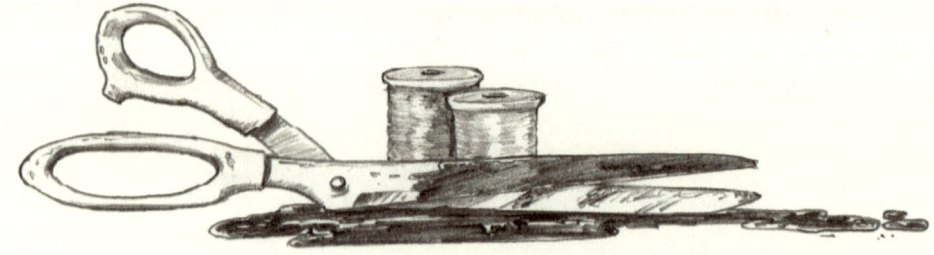

Sweet Water From the Rock
by
T. Lee Harris

Jars jumped as Étaín ingen Diarmata brought her wooden pestle down on the dried lichen in her mortar harder than was absolutely necessary.

"Pagan, am I?" She growled, giving the pestle a good grind and enjoying the cracking crunch as the plant disintegrated under her onslaught. "Don't believe in God? This woman is absolutely brainless! Of course I believe in God! Who else made the useful things of this world?"

"Have mercy, Mistress Dyer, surely the poor plant can't have offended so much."

Étaín stopped in mid-pound and turned to find Father Muiredach standing in the doorway to her workshop. The tall spare figure seemed lost in the loose, black robes and his cap of rusty curls caught the rays of the late morning sun to become a halo of flame. She treated him to a wry glance. "You're well aware the offender isn't here in my mortar, Father, or you wouldn't be here at this hour of a Monday. You've doubt-less heard about my difficulty with the new Abbess."

He lowered himself onto the long bench by the door without invitation and arranged his gangly limbs with a groan, then grinned, making his freckled face look even more boyish. "I have. I'll wager most of Clonbur has heard of it by now." The grin dimmed as he shifted position. "You wouldn't have any more of that Ladies' Bedstraw salve lying around? My joints are aching like an affliction of Job."

"It's God's blessing you had such a light touch of the fever, or you'd have more than a few aches as much as you chase round the countryside. I'm done with telling you to rest."

"I can't rest from my vocation."

"And what about *my* vocation? If you've come to pour oil on troubled waters, you might as well save your breath, Muiredach. Her high-and-mighty holiness has made it more than clear where she stands. Am I less a Christian than you because I practice the old healing ways? Your own mother was a dyer and a healer as well – it was she who taught my sisters and me the craft when she fostered us after our own parents died."

He made a placating gesture. "Peace! I'm not the enemy and neither is Abbess Humilia. Remember, she isn't from these parts—isn't even Irish; she simply doesn't understand how things are done here."

"She certainly didn't turn her English nose up at the altar cloths my sisters and I gave to the church! That was some of the richest crimson and purple you'll see for a long time. It took weeks to get the colors just so for the glory of God and just as long for Brigit and Aife to weave and embroider the cloth. How are we thanked? Just as it's going spring from a hard winter and all my supplies are low, I'm forbidden to gather my medicines and dyestuffs from holy ground lest I defile it with my 'pagan' presence. And not just me! My sisters, too! Well if Abbess Humilia wants any more of that purple...." Sweeping her hand to take in the depleted medicine shelves, she tipped over the mortar, spilling ground lichen over the surface of the workbench. "Oh look what I've done now! That's the last of the Corcair I have. Without it no one will have any more of that purple and unless I want to trek all the way to Scotland, the only place to get more...."

"...is on the stones of the old abbey garden walls." Shaking his head, he pleaded: "Étaín , give Abbess Humilia time...."

"Time? To do what? See my sisters into their graves and me out of a livelihood?"

Muiredach rose with effort to help her sweep the spill back into the mortar. She watched his stiff movements, then got an earthenware jar with an unbroken wax seal from a shelf, pressed it into his hand and sternly ordered him back to the bench.

He eased himself onto the planks again and ventured: "I'm sure the abbess sounded harsher than she intended, she'll change her attitude when she gets to know you and the people of the town better."

The healer simply raised an eyebrow and went back to grinding. He didn't blame her, it sounded lame even to him. It did not require a long acquaintance with the Abbess to learn she rarely changed her views on anything.

They lapsed into companionable silence as she worked, grinding the lichen into a fine powder and storing it carefully in a stoppered flask. It brought back good memories of helping his mother with this part of the work and he found the rhythm of it comforting. Étaín mixed another batch of ointment, blending the Ladies' Bedstraw into a measure of wool fat, but as she took an empty jar from the storage cabinet under the table it fell from her hands and bounced across the packed earth floor. It came to a halt against Father Muiredach's sandaled feet; he scooped it up and handed it to her. "Maybe you should heed your own advice, Étaín, you escaped the fever this winter, but you've worn yourself out caring for those who weren't so fortunate. You need to rest as well."

"I won't deny it. The burden will lighten when Brigit and Aife are well enough to help again. It was a sore blow to have both of them taken ill at the same time."

"It shouldn't be long, then. If Brigit feels well enough to be back at her loom, she must truly be on the mend, God be praised."

Étaín set the half-filled ointment jar down with a thump. "Oh, she never is!"

"But she is! I was just by the cottage and she already had the warp half-strung. She told me Fergal the shepherd set the loom up for her."

Hands a blur of movement, she hurriedly pulled off her work apron then tossed several jars and bunches of dried herbs into her basket. "Stubborn thing! I knew I couldn't trust her to stay abed. I have to get over there. Muiredach, can you close the workshop up for me?"

Not waiting for an answer, she bolted out, then reappeared around the doorframe admonishing: "And don't go peeking at the dyeing. If you make that lot go uneven, I'll have your hide, priest or no." She disappeared again and her footsteps had died away before the bemused priest stood, brushed off his habit and set about closing shutters. "Stubborn seems to run in the family."

Brigit wasn't at her loom when Étaín burst through the cottage door. She was busy stirring diced turnip into a cooking pot, her fresh-washed hair curling in a rose-gold cloud making her face more pointed and elfin as she beamed at her sister. "I expected you earlier! Muiredach must've made a few stops before he got to the workshop."

"No, he simply took his sweet time before mentioning you were up and about. Just what do you think you're doing?"

"Oh, don't fuss. I'm making stew with the piece of mutton Fergal brought us this morning."

"Brought to Aife more like, that lad's hopelessly besotted with her.

No matter, it was a kind thought and God knows we can all do with a bit of meat. There's been little enough of it this winter." She busied herself taking jars out of her willow basket. "How is she?"

"Sleeping. I gave her the last of the sleeping draught this morning. Considering I fell ill first and my fever only just broke, she's about due to come out of it."

"You're likely right, but I brought more of the sleeping draught and fever tonic, just the same."

Brigit put the spoon aside and perched on a stool pulled close to the hearth, arranging her skirts away from the open flame. "Fergal said he'd heard a rumor you and Abbess Humilia had a disagreement today."

"By all the saints, Father Muiredach is right, the whole of Clonbur *does* know!"

"Fergal also heard she labeled us all pagans and as such we've been banned from the Abbey grounds to gather herbs."

Étaín busied herself hanging the dried bunches from her basket.

Watching her sister's furious movements was answer enough and Brigit continued angrily: "Whoever gave her the name Humilia? If there's anything humble about that woman, I've yet to see it."

Étaín finished with the herbs and turned to jab at the bubbling stew with the spoon. "Well-named or no, her family is wealthy enough. The amounts they've put into rebuilding the abbey boggles the mind. It's a bit worrisome, too."

"The Danes?"

"Yes, the Danes. Now *there's* pagans for you. It hasn't been all that long since they came through and plundered the old abbey, and they did far worse to Galway. I'm told they left nothing standing down there. Rebuilding the abbey and church glorifies God, yes, but it could also attract the attention of the Danes."

"Maybe that's the whole idea."

"What?"

"Think about it, you have a daughter like her Holiness, what do you do with her? Shove her into wimple and veil, ship her off to another country, then call the Danes to get her. It's what I'd do if she were my kin."

"Brigit! Don't say such things!"

"You're laughing, though."

"I am not."

She was.

Brigit grinned with wicked glee, then returned to the problem at hand: "If we're banned from the abbey grounds, what will we do? There are things that can only be found there."

"We'll just have to find another source."

Before Brigit could respond, there came a light tap at the door; Étaín opened it to find Father Muiredach. He looked relieved to see her. "Praise God, you're still here. I've just been to see Ewain the harper and his family. His youngest is down again with the fever; he and his wife are at the point of distraction."

"Not young Broccan! Why is it the gentle ones are hit the hardest?"

"Perhaps because they have to be pushed farther before they'll fight back. I told Ewain we'd be over right away."

"I'll get my basket."

The boy's fever raged until well into the night and Father Muiredach, being Mass priest for the abbey, had left early on in order to be back at the church to officiate over the services. The abbey's bell was sounding for Nocturnes by the time Étaín stumbled home and into her bed. The child would live, but her medicines were more depleted than ever, so by daybreak she was ascending the hills above Clonbur and by the time of Terce, was well into unfamiliar territory and too far away to hear the bell ring. She'd found little of use to her.

She sank onto a stone clenched in the roots of a towering oak. It was easier to speak boldly of finding another source than it was to actually find that place; still she'd hoped to find a few more plants than she had. Most of what she'd gathered were common herbs, many of which already grew in her own small garden. She had yet to come across the rare ones; well, rare meant hard to find and sitting on a stone under a tree wouldn't bring them to her.

Resolute, she rose and turned deciding which way to go when she glimpsed a whorl of wispy, almost threadlike leaves in the bracken by a dry creek bed. Ladies' Bedstraw! Not only was it a fine medicine and one she was nearly out of, but its roots made a fiery crimson. Not quite as good as Corcair and it wouldn't go into the purple, but it was a good find. She pulled her belt knife and fell to work digging out the clump taking care not to damage any of the precious roots, then with the greater portion of the plant in her basket, looked beyond where she dug into the creek bed itself. The creek had been dry for quite a while, its rocks and pebbles giving way to mossy patches interspersed with grasses and bramble. Here and there in the scrub, she caught glimpses of more of the plants she sought. Sitting back on her heels, she breathed a few words of thanks, then stepped down into the dry bed and followed it, gathering and humming blissfully.

The creek bed brought her to a clearing and into a grove of ancient trees. She gazed with wonder at the mossy trunks, naming them off to herself and stopped abruptly, realizing that all twenty trees and plants of the Ogham, the ancient alphabet of her people, were growing here. Her delight at the discovery faded as she became aware of the complete silence in the grove, with not so much as an insect buzzing. The unnatural stillness chilled her in a way that even the bright sunlight pouring into the clearing couldn't touch. She suddenly knew where she was.

Neither she nor anyone she knew had actually been here, but she'd heard enough tales throughout her life that she should have recognized it as soon as she saw the Ogham trees. This grove was reputed to be haunted or worse—under a dreadful curse.

She hovered uncertainly at the edge of the grove, fingering the rosary in her pocket. This was supposed to be a cursed place…yet, all those medicinal herbs, trees and mosses….

It was then she saw it. It was nothing more than a mottled smudge on the sheer rockface towering over a smallish, bracken-covered hillock on the far side of the grove, but from where she stood, it looked like Corcair.

She was across the clearing and picking her way around boulders before she thought about what she was doing. As she drew closer, she saw that the lichen growing on the rocks was indeed the precious purple-making one. She stepped up onto the mound, but the matted weeds and brambles gave way under her. Her basket and carry bags were flung aside as darkness swallowed her and she slid, bounced and skidded in a cascade of branches and rubbish into a dark and dank place.

When she stopped, she lay still for a moment assessing damages, then deciding she wasn't dead, sat up to take stock of her surroundings. She couldn't see much of it. It appeared to be some kind of cave; there was water dripping somewhere further into the darkness. Clambering to her feet, she ventured a look at the way she came. Although it was bright daylight outside, very little light filtered through the matted undergrowth she fell through and it had sprung back into its prior position. She felt the ramp she'd fallen down and was surprised to feel steps there. They were well worn, but definitely a staircase.

"I better have some light before I do anything. God knows if there are any more steps around here. If there are, I don't care to find them the same way I found these." Touch told her that her skirts were a shambles and grimacing at the thought of further damage, she sliced a strip off the hem with her belt knife, wrapping it and some dried grasses around the end of a decent-sized branch that had fallen in with her. She struck a spark to the makeshift torch with the tinderbox from her scrip. It wouldn't burn very well without oil, but it was the best she could manage. Wrinkling her nose, she fanned smoke away, coughing: "Burning wool smells to high heaven, but at least I can see a little better."

The first step she took sent something metal that glinted and chimed across the stone floor. She stooped to retrieve it and was enchanted to see a man's gold wristband wrought in intricate knot designs. Her enchantment turned quickly to horror as she looked beyond and found a pile of human bones. "Oh, heavens, I've fallen into a tomb!"

After reverently placing the wristband atop the piled bones, and offering a prayer for the souls of the dead, she stopped. "But if this is a tomb, why aren't the bones laid out instead of piled higglety-pigglety. And where is the seal? There ought to be stones to seal the entrance and I don't see any..." She turned to look for the stones and found herself nose to nose with a snarling beast.

With a yelp, she leapt back, landing in ankle-deep icy water and brought the sputtering torch around like a fiery club. It struck the beast across the snout, sending sparks in all directions. She crouched in the shallow pool, heart pounding waiting for the creature to spring. It didn't move; after a moment she saw why. "God be praised, it's a statue."

Gulping air to slow her still-racing heart, she stepped out of the cold water with a sense of disgust at both wet shoe leather and her sudden fear. Being used as a club had done her torch no good, either. Urging its abused tip into higher flame, she crept in for a closer look at

the hideous thing. It was no use; the torch was flickering more than ever as well as dropping sparks and embers on her.

"I'm never going to find out what's what with this feeble thing." Staring at the stone floor, she reached a decision. "Obviously, I'm not going to do the truly intelligent thing and run screaming for home, so let's do this properly."

With what was left of the torch jammed into a crack in the wall, and using another branch for a broom, she cleaned a patch of floor in the middle of the room for a small fire. The floor turned out to be fitted flagstone, and clearing debris revealed a large bronze and enamel disc set into the floor. It had been chopped apart with something like an axe. Part of the disc as well as the surrounding stone was missing, but the design seemed to depict a snake. That was a new one. In all the stories the harper had sung, only the stories of Saint Patrick dealt with snakes and this place was surely much older than that.

As she coaxed her fire along, she was pleased to see that the opening through which she'd fallen drew like a chimney. At least she'd not be troubled with the place filling with smoke. Satisfied, she turned her attention to the cavern. It was once a natural cavern, but had been extensively reworked in ancient times, expanded and squared off with four evenly spaced square pillars for added support. It wasn't as big as she'd at first thought, maybe it had been originally, but now, the far end was closed off with a masonry wall that was crumbling under the invasion of tree roots from the grove above.

Small stones shifted behind her and she whirled to find nothing there, then realized she'd been hearing scraping and rustling for a while. Mice most likely—or rats, the nasty dirty things. It would be the first sign of life she'd seen in this place, come to think of it. There hadn't even been any spiders. She was grateful for that, she didn't much like spiders.

The firelight picked out shallow carved figures along the wall, putting thoughts of rodents out of her head. Starting at the stairway there was a frieze of stylized warriors engaged in fierce battle. "Not a tomb, I think. It looks more like old Ewain's songs about the ancient religions. Some kind of temple, perhaps?"

At the end of the frieze, she found the source of the water. It oozed from a badly damaged fountain in the wall that looked as if it had once been an ornate green man, now hacked and shattered like the bronze disk on the floor, the copper pipe that brought the water twisted and almost closed. Water seeped through cracks in the bent pipe and through places where the years had eaten the soft metal away. It ran across the floor and pooled in the area just in front of the snarling statue.

All this destruction was deliberate, but what would it accomplish? She went back to the statue. It was a limestone carving of a wolf or lion with its front paws resting on two severed human heads, its teeth bared in a vicious snarl, clenching a severed arm. Beside it lay the mound of bones intermixed with bits of armor, rusty weapons and here and there the glint of gold—but no skulls. Looking up, she found them. Directly over the beast a triangular area of small niches was carved into the wall. Every niche was occupied by a human skull.

"A skull rack. It's a temple, then. I've heard plenty about this kind of place, and it's time enough to put distance between me and it." Curiosity satisfied, she turned intending to douse the fire and head back into sunlight and fresh air and froze as still as the stone beast at what she saw. There was a gigantic snake between herself and the stairs. It was reared up, so large that its head almost touched the ceiling. This was not a statue.

She pressed back against the sculpture hoping her involuntary gasp wasn't as loud as it sounded to her. The snake seemed to be ignoring her and moving toward the brightly burning fire. Étaín forgot her fear and watched in amazement as the huge serpent slowly and sluggishly coiled itself onto the flames. It drew the fire into itself and although the once burning branches were now cold, the chamber was still brightly lit. The light now radiated from the snake whose scales glowed like hot bronze and its eyes shone like backlit carnelian disks. It all but sighed in pleasure, then turned its burning eyes to her.

Feeling her way, she edged in the opposite direction. The serpent moved back into her path and sampled the air with its forked tongue. She got the distinct impression it was laughing at her.

In the blink of an eye, it lunged; she launched herself flat across the floor and landed beside the statue. The snake splashed into the pool of cold water, then reared back with a hiss of pain. Scales dropped where the water touched it and the skin beneath looked crackled like the surface of a half-burned log. It lashed out in blind fury, its massive tail shattering one of the support columns like a sliver of glass. The stones of the ceiling groaned, raining dust and grit.

The bronze head swung around and located her again. It struck at her and she rolled behind the statue, fearing she'd be crushed as the ancient carving rocked and shattered under the impact. Skulls pelted her as the shaken rack emptied itself. Suddenly, thick smoke rose from the shattered skulls to swirl and solidify before her eyes into seven men.

Well, she'd really done it now. Not only was a demon from hell wanting to crunch her bones, but she'd also angered the ancient dead. She gripped her rosary and prepared for her inevitable fate.

Her praying fingers froze on the beads as the spirit warriors turned from her and advanced silently on the serpent. Hissing with rage, the snake tried to brush the shadow men away. Its tail passed through them carrying streamers of mist with it as it smashed another column instead.

Étaín crouching behind the remains of the stone beast, felt a cold touch and looked fearfully up into the painted face of a shadow warrior. He gestured toward the stairs. Stones dropped from the roof and he gestured again, more urgently. Without a word, she bolted for the way out, scrambling up the stairs with rubble pelting her from the collapsing structure.

She didn't stop running until she fell across the roots of a gnarled rowan. She was never sure if she tripped on the roots or if the tremor when the old temple gave way knocked her down. Whichever, as she watched, the hillock and part of the surrounding rock disappeared into a deep hole. It took a while for things to stop crashing and shifting. When all was finally quiet, she crept to the edge of the destruction. Nothing visible remained of the ancient stones, but the sound of running water rose above all. In the middle of the tumbled rock, a clear spring bubbled up. It quickly pooled and she knew before long, there would be a new well and its overflow would once again fill the dry creek bed she'd followed to find this place.

As she leaned to watch the cleansing water dance in the sunlight, she felt an odd texture to the stone under her hand. There was lichen covering the rock and growing over the tumbled stones encircling the pool. It was Corcair.

Étaín picked her way back down the hillside to the sound of birdsong and running water. Her basket and full carry bags thudded against her sides with every step she took. A fine lot, she should be able to do a deal of good with these.

Nursing a Grudge
by
Ginny Fleming

Jolene was exhausted. She'd brought the new baby home from the hospital a mere two weeks prior, and he'd not yet slept through three hours straight. The first week hadn't been so bad. Michael, her husband, wisely scheduled a vacation to begin the night of little Tim's birth, and he'd graciously taken the middle of the night feedings that first week. He gave the baby a bottle of pumped breast milk to tide him over until the early morning, at which time a bedraggled Jolene would drag herself from the warm bed and nod off again, sitting up at the breakfast table, with the suckling baby attached to her body like a tiny voracious parasite.

But even on the mornings of the first week, Michael was clueless. "Jolene, you look like someone on a forced death march," he joked, "didn't you get any sleep last night? Heck, me and the Tim-Man did a two o'clock and a four-thirty boogie last night, and I still managed to get a few hours beauty sleep."

Upon hearing these words of pseudo-sympathy, Jolene remembered very much wanting to throw her orange juice at the man she'd just nine months before swore to love and cherish until death do them part. And now, over seven days later, she still seethed at the memory of Michael's clucking.

On the second Monday morning following the baby's birth, she stood at the picture window in the living room and watched her big, strong, rested husband pull out of the driveway and make his escape, back to his job in the big city. She glanced down at Timmy. He'd detached himself from his morning manna and dozed with the sleep of the sated, his tiny mouth in a bow, tasteful memories causing him to continue sucking in his slumber. "Tim, if he only knew..." she whispered to her son, while carrying him to his crib, hoping for an hour— at least, enough time to grab a shower and cup of decaf.

As she placed the sleeping baby on his back (a prevention against SIDS), she smiled. Surely, this will pass, she thought, surely things will get better... *But, what about the dreams?* These last words came to her thoughts unbidden, unwelcome guests in the early morning sunlight. *Don't you think you should tell Michael about the dreams?*

"Yeah, right," she whispered aloud, "like he'd understand. It must be a man-thing, being able to operate with little or no sleep. Or perhaps, it's just a Michael-thing. Either way, if I told him about the dreams, he'd bust a gut laughing... No," she closed the door on her sleeping son, "Michael doesn't need to know." She wrapped her mind around the fleeting thought of keeping the matter of the dreams to herself, and turned into the hallway, intent upon reaching her goal of a (still) early morning shower, when out of the corner of her eye, something moved. Darkness. A shadow. A wisp. Nothing more.

She giggled (her first impulse— she always giggled when frightened, had giggled when fearful ever since she was a little girl— until the tears would join the hysterical laughter). The giggles died down and she rubbed her eyes. "Wasted days and wasted nights," she murmured. Reaching for the easy answer, Jolene hoped a shower would wash away the troubled night.

Turning on the hot water, she stepped gratefully into the warm sprinkles. For the first few moments, she stood stock still, allowing the water to hit her face and run in hot rivulets down her weary, still slightly bloated body. Finally, she roused herself and picked up the terry washcloth from the tub rack. Soon, a satisfying lather joined the hot water cascading down from the showerhead, and Jolene felt herself relaxing.

All at once, she heard/felt something move in the north corner of the bathroom, and for one insane second, she wondered if Michael had doubled back and returned home. *Perhaps for one more coffee-kiss? Right. Coffee-kisses are on hold for the time being.*

Peering around the steam-fogged shower curtain, Jolene scanned the bathroom, knowing with a certainty she was totally alone in the shower-humid room. She giggled. "You're crazier than a three dog night..." with another chuckle, she returned to the luxury of her soapy shower. "A few more nights of no sleep and I'll be seeing Elvis wearing my Victoria's Secret... Well, if I can't wear it, at least the King should get the benefits of my Wonder Bra... the Wonder is, I Wonder when I'll be able to squeeze back into it..." she chuckled again, this time, not really so amused.

She knew Wonder-Bras were not the heavy concern troubling her mind. She also knew if she only reached a little farther, she might actually remember the exact words she'd been hearing in the fevered and frantic dreams that passed for sleep. A small fuzzy memory told her there'd been someone or something whispering about... *the baby. What was it saying about the baby?* She didn't remember. She didn't want to remember.

"I'm just tired." She stated this hollow judgment to the steamy room, as she stepped dripping from the shower. Wrapping herself in the jumbo-sized fluffy towel, and turbaning her wet hair in a smaller matching towel, she left the bathroom. Battling the urge to return to bed, she dressed in yellow sweats and pulled a comb through her shoulder length dark hair.

"Step it up, Jo!" she berated herself, glancing at the dust ruffle trailing around the bottom of the queen-sized bed (Why did she feel such a black dread looking at the cheery ruffle with the delicate white fabric decorated by lavender sprigs? No... Not the ruffle... It was—), "Step it up, Woman!" she growled, with a false harshness designed to drag her attention from the dreaded dust ruffle, "Timmy won't sleep long, and I want my coffee! Jeez, I can't believe I'm actually looking forward to decaf coffee..."

She managed two sips of the non-zippy brown brew when the pre-ten A.M. morning stillness was split by the baby's bleating shrieks. "The master calls," she sighed.

Returning to the nursery, Jolene marveled at the tiny enraged warrior, his open mouth quivering in his lung-filled canopy of indignant fury. "My, my," she soothed, checking his diaper, "such a little man to raise such a big fuss." After a swift clean up, during which Timmy tracked his Mommy with his eyes (though Jolene knew, or thought she did, her new-born wasn't really focusing yet), she lifted him from his Pooh-decorated crib and automatically raised her shirt for her ravenous son. Her nipples were a little sore, but the feeding eased the ache in her swollen breasts, and she smiled with the relief of Timmy's insistent nursing.

With her left hand, she picked up the remote and queued the CD player and the soothing sound of Enya flowed from the speakers in the corner of the living room. She relaxed into an antique rocker, its padded seat and back a comfort to her sleep-deprived achy body. Minutes into the nursing, Jolene drifted off.

"*...and the baby is mine....*" these words spoken into the fuzzy mixture of Enya combined with a sticky dream caused her to jerk awake, separating Timmy from his grasp on her right breast. His raging showed his anger at his Mother's apparent disregard for his welfare and Jolene quickly reinserted Timmy's world back into his toothless maw.

"Jeez-Louise, Tim-Tim!" she breathed, "Don't have a cow, Man!" She ended this witty remark with a cascade of giggles and repeated, "Yeah, don't have a cow. That's my job." She wished she could continue the laughter long enough to actually feel happy, but the words that woke her sat like a lead sinker on her mind. "*...and the baby is mine....*"

A cold chill ran down her back and she shuddered. "A sugar drop," she muttered, turning to the once again sleeping baby, "better grab some cheese and crackers or your mommy will be sprawled out on the floor. And we wouldn't want that, would we, Timmy-Boy?" She carried the feeding/sleeping infant into the kitchen, retrieved the cheese from the refrigerator and the crackers from the pantry in a one-handed ballet. "A little snack on the run. Right, Tim?" She munched the Colby cheese and soda crackers while standing at the kitchen counter. Suddenly, she caught a wisp of something out of the corner of her eye, bringing her attention to the large stone crock that doubled as a waste container. The shadow had settled at the bottom left of the beige-glazed antique and disappeared into the wall.

"Strange..." Jolene muttered aloud, "I don't remember reading in my pregnancy prep-books about one's *eyesight* being affected by pregnancy." She returned her attention to her still uneaten cheese. "Sleep. More sleep," she declared between bites, "that's the answer."

Michael returned home two hours after darkness settled over the subdivision to find Jolene sprawled across the bed, her nursing bra open, Timmy by her side, growing fretful, his tiny arms and legs wildly bicycling, unable to get a purchase on his (seemingly) constant meal. Lifting his squirming son from the bed, Michael shook his head in disdain, glaring down at his sleeping wife.

"Jolene!" he spoke harshly, while using his free hand to roughly shake the snoring woman, drool trailing down her open mouth, pooling on the whiteness of the pillowcase. "Jolene, wake up!" he demanded. "What do you think you're doing?"

She didn't come up from sleep easily. Waking was like climbing from a cold, dark hole, its sides slick with sleep sweat. "...don't take the baby... not the baby..." she mumbled.

"*Of course* I'm taking the baby," Michael growled. "It's a wonder you didn't roll over on `im." He stalked from the room and headed for the nursery, leaving Jolene stunned, rubbing her eyes.

"What?" she croaked, finding her voice among the dust bunnies of her mind. "What are you talking about? Michael? What's going on?" It seemed she weighed a ton as she pulled her sweaty-numb body from the warmth of the rumpled bed. She padded on bare feet into the nursery following after her husband and son. "Will you please tell me what's wrong?"

Michael paused beside the crib, Timmy still held to his chest, his large hand cradling the baby's head, "*What's wrong?!?*" he repeated her words putting a hiss in his voice. "I'll tell you what's wrong!! I come home after a long day's work to find my wife passed out cold on the bed, my little boy helpless beside her! Jo, I'm the one who should be asking what's wrong! What's wrong with you? Is there something wrong with you?"

Jolene giggled. *I must be scared*, she thought. "No... Michael. No," she shook her head and reached out to take Timmy from him. "Nothing's wrong. I'm just tired. Needed a nap. That's all." Her outstretched arms were met with apathy. It seemed he held the baby tighter, if that were possible. "Give him to me," she whispered.

"No." He spoke flatly, leaving no room for discussion. "You're tired. Go back to bed. I'll take care of my son." Michael turned his back to Jolene and placed Timmy into his crib, cooing at the infant and checking his diaper with a brave finger.

Jolene shook her head and mumbled, "Have it your way, Burger King. Won't do any good to go back to bed. Can't sleep—"

"Seemed you were doing a good job of it," Michael interrupted her, "sawing them off pretty damn good, if you ask me." He fastened the tape on the side of the Mickey Mouse decorated plastic diaper. "Is Mommy boozin' it up while Daddy's at work, Tim-Man? Is Mommy a boozer?" he whiddled at the baby, "Well, is she? Fess up, Tim-Man. You know I'll find the empties, don't ya—"

"Shut up, Michael," she growled, "that's no way to talk to the baby."

Michael grinned. "You know I'm just kidding, don't ya, Jo? Sweetheart— Just go back to bed. I'll give Tim a bottle."

"Told you I can't sleep." She threw up her hands, showing her defeat in the 'Give Me The Baby' battle. "I'll go fix supper. You're probably hungry—"

"Don't bother," Michael interrupted her and lifted the baby from his crib. "I grabbed something on the way home." He cradled the infant in his muscular arms and carried him towards the kitchen to warm a pre-pumped bottle.

"Who is she?" Jolene demanded at his kitchen-bound back.

This time it was Michael who giggled. "Are you crazy?" he asked. "Can't a guy stop for a bite with a few friends on the way home without getting accused of adultery?"

"Sure." She grabbed the bottle from the refrigerator, slamming the door just a little bit too hard. "Sure. A guy can stop off with a few friends. If the few friends number more than one."

"I'm gonna ask you one more time," he snapped "*Are you crazy?*"

She likewise slammed the microwave door too hard. "You're gonna ask me that one too many times, Michael. Tell me. Do you ask her that?"

He stared at her with a vacant expression. When he finally spoke, it was with an inflection she'd never heard him use before. "For your information," he said quietly. "She is one of my partners. We're working on a very important project and my taking time off for you has put us behind."

"For me? For me?!? I thought you took off to see your son brought into this world!" She didn't intend to practically scream the words with such venom.

"You know what I mean."

She shook her head at him, handing him the warmed bottle, "Yeah... I think I do." Wiping her damp hands on the dishtowel beside the sink, she turned quickly and added over her shoulder, "Goin' back to bed. Looks like you've got things in hand in here."

The night seemed two nights long. She lay beside her sleeping husband eyes wide open, staring through the darkness at the ceiling. Michael's even breathing testified to the fact he was deeply asleep.

"Creep," she whispered at his back. "You'll get yours, Bud. Some day, you'll get yours. Just wait til you get so tired you see things.... And hear things. Then I'll be the one asking: *Are you crazy?* Well, Michael? *Are*—"

Her ranting whispers were interrupted by a not so subtle rustling under the bed.

"Are we having fun yet?" asked the dark thing that slithered from under the lavender sprigged dust ruffle. "Man! I'm gettin' tired of waitin' for you to fall asleep. Ain't it a bitch when you try and try and it just doesn't come? Kinda like ole' Michael, there, when he's had a few brews too many. I'm sorry," it apologized (though Jolene doubted its sincerity). "I shouldn't have brought up Michael's *short-comings*, so to speak. He's never *that way* with her."

Jolene giggled; a high pitched giggle that she tried to hold in, even to the point of holding her mouth with both hands, but to no avail. Tiny snippits of guilty frightened laughter escaped between her trembling fingers. Michael mumbled something from his sleep that sounded like: "...touch me there... no... not there..."

"Creep," Jolene whispered at his back.

The dark thing (that resembled Jolene's strange Uncle Myron with its sparse tuffs of hair-like fur sticking out over what passed for ears— She noted the resemblance and a new set of giggles erupted— a few from simple humor. Himself, Uncle Myron, bore a strong resemblance to Yoda, the wizened little creature from Star Wars) slithered farther out from under the bed and now crawled towards the open bedroom door. Turning back toward the woman who watched from the bed, her hands clasped to her betraying mouth, the creature smiled. Jolene's giggles died in her throat.

"It's time," it said, "time for Timmy."

"No," Jolene whispered.

This time, it was the dark thing that giggled, but the woman didn't get the joke. It pointed an obscenely long finger towards the bed and ordered, "Follow me."

She didn't want to. Every fiber of her body, and quite a few morsels of her inner being fought against the wishes of the dark thing beckoning her from the bedroom's doorway. But, within seconds she felt herself pulling the blanket back and rising from the bed. "Creep," she

whispered at Michael's back as she followed the 'Uncle Myron' thing to the nursery doorway.

"No," Jolene whispered again.

"Yes." said the dark thing. It pointed at the crib, visible in a shaft of moonlight through the open doorway. "Time for Timmy," it repeated, and giggled once more.

"You can't make me."

This time, the vile creature stopped in mid-slither/crawl and winked at her in the moonlight. "Ahh! But I can!" it chortled, "I can make you do *anything*. I can make you pull the trigger on the gun you hold to your head. I can make you jump as you stand on the ledge high above the cold hard sidewalk below. I can make you—"

"You can't make me hurt my baby." Jolene stated matter-of-factly.

"Ahh! *But I can!*" it repeated, "I can, cause I'm what lives under your bed. You fear me. And right you should!"

"I *don't* fear you," she lied, but a single giggle made its way over her cold lips.

It chortled, "Everybody fears me. *I'm darkness*. I'm what goes bump. Watch what I can do!" It pointed at her and she felt her hands move unbidden.

She skipped up to the side of the crib, feeling the muscles of her legs jerk with the child-like motion, but registering an alien detachment with her body. She watched her hands reach out for her sleeping baby, and wondered at the tiny weight she cradled to her breast. "No," she whispered, violently shaking her head at the thing leering up at her, it's clawed hands gripping the bed-slats on the Pooh-decorated crib. "No...."

"Yessss..." cooed the dark thing, "the baby is mine."

"No! Don't make me do this thing! Please!" she pleaded, her hand shaking, inches from Timmy's pink bow-shaped mouth.

"You want an out?" wheedled the darkness holding onto the cheerful crib, "I said— *do you want an out?*"

Jolene trembled with the effort of keeping her hand from the child's face, "Yes!!" she hissed, "*Please, God!*"

"Don't 'Please-God' me," snickered the thing that lived under the bed. "Nothing in this vast universe will 'Please-God' me... nothing, that is, except the breath of your first-born. But, there *is* an out."

Jolene felt bile rise in her throat as she croaked the words that she knew down deep in her troubled heart would damn her immortal soul. "Tell me," she whispered. A single tear fell from her eye, but she managed not to giggle. "Tell me my out."

On the sixteenth day since giving birth to the most perfect baby in the whole wide world, Jolene awoke from her early morning slumber and glanced down at tiny Timmy, with the wispy blond hair (so like his handsome father), cradled in her arms, suckling in his sleep. Beside her in the bed, Michael lay with his back to her. Still. Dead to the world.

Night Thoughts
by
Mary Gehant-Lagunez

A dark fog is rising,
There's a scream in the night;
A mysterious stranger
Appears in my sight.

Somebody's creeping
Up my stair.
But I live alone—
So who is there?

Sirens are wailing
And a gunshot rings out.
A man with a pipe says
The game is afoot.

My friends are nearby
While I'm snug in my bed.
What does it matter if I've
Dark thoughts in my head?

Yes, Edgar and Agatha,
Ngaio, Arthur, Josephine,
And let's not forget
Mr. Ellery Queen.

They're here, stacked on the table.
I read 'em all whenever I'm able.

Truth in a Tale
by
Marian Allen

An excerpt from UNICORN RISING, Book Two of the SAGE series.

Nerissa is a child of ten, a runaway slave who now works as a menial for Tartarus, a disagreeable and solitary fisherman. Farukh, a popular storyteller, has invited himself to stay the night, much to Tartarus' disgust.

"Shall I tell you a story about Tortoise?" the storyteller asked, when Nerissa was done clearing away supper.

Nerissa nodded, her heart thudding with joy. This would be the first complete story she had ever heard from Farukh. And all for her. Only for her. (Tartarus hardly counted.)

"I'll tell you two. One is true and one is false. You tell me which is which."

Nerissa wiped her mouth on her arm, her hands on the skirt of her ragged dress.

Farukh began:

Once, my child, there were a brother and sister. The sister was your age; the brother, a year or two older. Now, these children were neither more nor less naughty than most, but one night.... One night, the brother heard the girl crying in terror and woke to see Tortoise crawling across the floor toward her.

"Stop!" the boy shouted.

"The girl is mine," said Tortoise (for, being a Spirit Animal, he could speak).

"Of course," said the boy. "But I happen to know that my sister has a full day of mischief planned tomorrow. Why take a little nip now and a little nip then, when you can wait and take a mouthful tomorrow night."

"I'm hungry now," Tortoise whined.

"Here's a piece of fish I was saving for my breakfast," said the boy, and Tortoise ate it and went away.

Nerissa laughed and hugged her knees.

       The next day, the sister really was a most shocking child, just as her brother had promised. That night, before she went to bed, the little girl's brother rubbed salt all over her left foot and told her to leave it sticking out of the covers.

       When Tortoise came, he took that salty foot in his mouth and the salt rubbed all over his tongue. He pulled back.

       "What's the matter?" asked the boy.

       "This is the saltiest child I ever tasted," said Tortoise. "Give me something to drink."

       The boy had a jug of wine he had told his sister to steal, and he gave it to Tortoise. Greedy as he is, he drained the whole bottle in one swig!

       Then, of course, he had to close his eyes for a little nap.

       "Quick," said the boy to his sister. "Hide behind that chair and give me your dress."

       The boy put his sister's dress on Tortoise's tail.

       "Wake up!" the boy cried. "She's trying to get away! She's behind you!"

       Tortoise woke up, hissed, and took one angry nip after another—out of his own tail!

Nerissa let go of her knees and held her sides, hooting with laughter.

"And that is why," said Farukh, "Tortoise's tail has a series of spikes on it: They aren't really spikes, they're all that's left after he got through with himself. They say the little girl was more careful after that. And so, perhaps, was Tortoise."

Nerissa clapped her hands until they were red.

"She'd be better off getting her rest than listening to that trash," said Tartarus.

"Now the other one!" said Nerissa. She realized what she had done—demanding, when she should have been imploring—and hung her head. She felt a hand laid softly on her crown, stroking her greasy hair, and she looked up into Farukh's sparkling blue eyes.

"I know who you've been keeping company with," he said, with his quick, bright smile. "I make allowances."

"Will you tell the other one?" she asked.

"Bah!" said Tartarus. "Why don't you get down on your belly and beg him, girl?"

Nerissa's hand went to the handle of the skillet beside her. Tartarus saw it and gave an evil grin. She let go and, lifting her nose into the air, turned away from him and back to Farukh.

"Please tell me the other one," she said.

"The other one.... It isn't pretty, child. It isn't funny."

But it was, Nerissa felt, important.

"Please," she said.

Yesterday—or was it a long time ago?—a sword was forged by a very special smith. He was a man born, as all men are, of a man and a woman, but he had, from birth, a strong communion with making and with metal. From time to time he would take some of his goods, muffled in cloth like so many men with identities to protect, to the Great Market in Granitz, the capital of Kozabir. There, a sword of this smith's making was bought by a mercenary, who called the sword a "she" and named her Freer of Souls.

Now you may know, child, that Tortoise is the patron Spirit of mercenaries. You may also know that Tortoise loves a sacrifice. To Tortoise, then, was Freer of Souls dedicated, and every life she took was called a sacrifice to him. In return for these gifts, the mercenary asked victory in combat.

After some years, the mercenary began to place himself in the thickest of any battle, to search for assignments that promised to be bloodiest, to give deliberate offense in order to goad other men to fight.

Then, during a border skirmish with another country, this mercenary found himself standing amid

the dead and dying of his enemies, and among the more lightly wounded.

"For Tortoise," he said, and proceeded to kill all the helpless living within his reach. When he was done, he moved and began again.

Suddenly, with no puff of smoke, no spark, no rush of wind, the Black Warrior stood before him.

Nerissa shivered. She had lost sight of the shack, of the dying sun outside, of the storyteller himself. What she saw was a field of murdered men, one man standing among them with a dripping sword, and a soldier in gleaming black armor facing him.

Do you know the Black Warrior, child? He is Tortoise when he takes a personal hand in a fight.

"This is for you, My Lord," said the mercenary. "Grant me glory. Grant me power."

The Black Warrior raised his sword.

"Defend yourself, slayer of wounded," said Tortoise.

"But this is for you!"

"Defend yourself. Force your claims against me."

"Grant me nothing, then, but accept my offering."

"A battle bravely fought is an offering to my taste," said the Black Warrior. "Murder never was."

And while the mercenary faced the Warrior, who was invisible to all but him, a man in the pay of the other country struck, and the mercenary from Granitz fell dead. The victor took Freer of Souls, cleaned her on her dead master's tunic, and replaced his own sword with her. He gave her another name and he used her more direly than her first owner ever had.

He didn't dedicate his killings to Tortoise, though, so Tortoise took no notice, but left him to fashion his own destruction.

Farukh sat back. "Now," he said, "which story was real, and which was false?"

Nerissa shook herself, feeling as if wisps of narrative still clung about her.

Behind her, Tartarus poked up the fire. "I'm not lighting the lamp." He closed the door on the night. "I've heard enough codswallop for one evening."

"Well, child?" said Farukh.

"The second one is true. The second one."

"Thought you didn't believe in Tortoise," Tartarus mocked.

"I believe the second one."

"Why?" asked Farukh.

"Tortoise, in the second one.... He isn't a fool. He's terrible, but he isn't a monster. And he doesn't belong to anybody."

Tartarus grunted in the darkness. "The girl isn't a total idiot," he said.

Monster of the Full Moon Night

By

George Lopez

Sherry tucked her purse and paper tightly under her arm. Once again, she stepped out onto the empty street and peered into the darkness. Still no bus in sight. Her wrist watch now read 10:45. She put it to her ear, then checked it again. Could it be fast? Shaking her head, she returned to the bench. Alone at the bus stop, she was sure the last bus ran at 10:00 PM, but no bus had been by in almost an hour. Now she wondered if the schedule had changed. She couldn't be sure and wished she had checked earlier. Sherry seldom rode the commuter busses and wouldn't have done so this time except that she had promised. Weeks ago, she gave her word when she said she would help at the hospital today. How could she have foreseen her car would be in the shop?

With tiny swirls of dust accompanying, a cool breeze danced a page of newspaper along the vacant sidewalk. Sherry pulled the wool collar of her coat up as it tumbled by. She shuddered and tried diverting her attention to browsing her newspaper. The street lamp offered a poor source of light. She could only make out bold headlines:

"FULL MOON MONSTER STILL AT LARGE!"

The story was one she really didn't want to read. Everyone in the Bay area was familiar with it. The last dead girl made number six on the killer's list. Like the others, this girl was sexually assaulted and then brutally mutilated. Sherry had overheard two nurses talking about it earlier.

"All the girls were attacked around midnight," said the taller woman. I'm not sure it's even a human. How could it be a human."

"I know," nodded her friend. "I read that the killer appears to use something sharp like a scalpel or straight razor."

"They say this monster always attacks on a full moon."

"Did you read about this last girl? She was loved by so many—"

"Isn't it just like that? The nice ones are always the ones we lose."

"I know what I would like done to the guy when they catch him."

"Don't get your hopes up. He'll never go to prison—he's insane."

"You realize that there's a full moon tonight?"

Sherry wanted to be home. She had planned being home well before midnight tonight. Perhaps the streets wouldn't feel so menacing if they weren't so deserted. A result of the migration from the cities, she told herself. But she didn't regret her own move to the suburbs. If only Ben were here. But, he never would have permitted her out like this. Ben protected her better than her own parents had in her childhood. She missed Ben as much now as she did when he died. Has it been four years already? Time certainly wasn't healing this wound for her. Perhaps it would have helped if she had started dating; not that she hoped to remarry.

A sweet fragrance wafted from her purse as she opened it. Fishing around inside it, she noticed the tiny powder-blue case of paste-perfume. It had a tiny crack along one edge. Next to it was a gold compact which she withdrew. The tiny mirror in it was barely helpful as she appraised her reflection. There were still only the tiniest signs of crow's-feet at the corners of her eyes. Actually, they enhanced her appearance. Yes, she was still a handsome woman. Perhaps men did find her attractive. Although she probably could never be a girlish size six again, she was still shapely. Maybe she should start dating—even though she knew it was unlikely she could ever find another Ben.

Dear Ben. He was not only her husband, he was her lover, her friend, and her guardian. Her knight in shining armor. An incredibly brilliant man, his white hair made him appear much older than her. He had already taken early retirement when they met. She was pleasantly surprised to discover how comfortably they could live on the royalties from his electronic creations. He even designed their home in the suburbs. The big house had all the modern conveniences of the city and all the charm of the country.

Even now, after he was gone, she still felt safe there. Her sound-proof study was virtually impenetrable. Locking the steel shutter-door of her study insured her safety. The electronic bolt required her hand-print to both enter or exit. Sherry could not imagine finding another man so clever and understanding.

Strolling home from a late dinner, Sherry had been frightened by a sinister group of men. To avoid them, she cut across his fenced property. But, in the dark, she fell into a construction excavation and could not climb out. He found her the next morning when he came out to watch the sun rise. Before he could even tell it was an attractive woman, he was obviously concerned about the welfare of the trapped being. He could have simply notified the authorities; after all, she was trespassing. But, instead, he provided her his hospitality. This included a chance to freshen up, and some of his clean clothes—afterwhich he saw to it she made it home safely. Soon after, they began seeing each other. They often joked about how he snared her for his wife, and how he din't throw her back and wait for something better.

Distant headlights interrupted Sherry's thoughts. She got up to investigate. Was this the bus at last? No, it was a car. As the vehicle slowly passed, the driver thoroughly surveyed her, making her feel very uncomfortable. Suddenly the car sped off as a white laundry van approached. The van passed quickly and two more cars followed shortly after. Sherry checked her watch again. It was almost 11:00 PM. What could have possibly happened to the bus?

Sherry began pacing in front of the bus stop. Now it would take a miracle for her to be off the streets before midnight. She swore she would never commit again; especially to conditions that could put her in such a dangerous predicament. As she watched for the bus, she saw her shadow stretch out on the street before her. She turned to see headlights coming from the other direction. The white van was returning. It stopped across the street from her.

"Mrs. Moore?" asked a polite voice from the van.

Sherry squinted to see the driver. "Yes?"

"Mrs. Moore. It's me, David. David Wilson. I deliver your laundry Ma'am."

"David?" Sherry remembered David. He had picked up laundry at her home for the past five years. Since before he was a teenager. "Aren't you working a little late, David?"

"No, Ma'am. The company lets me use the van—on account of my car breaking down and— Forgive me, Ma'am, but you shouldn't be out here alone like this."

"Yes I know, but the bus is late."

"No, Ma'am, the bus don't run on Saturday afternoons no more."

Sherry's spirit sank.

"Ma'am? Maybe I could give you a lift to where you can catch a cab. I'd drive you home, Ma'am, but I don't have gas money to come back on."

Sherry thought about getting home. She knew David. Maybe he could get her home before anything terrible might happen.

"You probably could get a cab at the hotel," he continued. "That's if Herb hasn't already gone."

"Herb?" Sherry crossed the street to the van.

"Yes, Ma'am. Herb's the cab driver. Or, you could call a friend, or even get a room. The commuter buses don't run again till Monday."

Sherry wrinkled her brow in thought. Then looking in her purse, she asked: "David, could you take me home if I give you $20."

"Yes Ma'am! I'd be glad to. I wish I didn't need the mon–"

"That's all right David," she interrupted, "I understand." Sherry hurried around to the passenger side of the van. There was only one seat in the van—the driver's. David quickly piled bags of laundry near the entry, apologizing as he devised a sitting place for her.

"Sorry about the seating arrangements Mrs. Moore. I think you might be more comfortable if you sit on these and lean against the side of the van."

Sherry climbed into the van and sat on the soft bags filled with laundry. She pulled futilely at her skirt, trying to maintain some dignity. Finally, she tucked her legs as best she could, and held on as the van pulled out.

"I'll try to drive slow so as you don't have a bad time of it."

"Please hurry David. I would feel better if I could be home quickly."

"I understand, Ma'am."

David soon turned onto the freeway and pressed on toward the suburbs where Sherry lived. She leaned back against the side of the van and closed her eyes. The van didn't tip and shake as much on the highway as it did on city streets. By car, she could be home in under a half hour. Soon she would be free of this terror.

"I sure was sorry to hear about Mr. Moore."

Sherry half opened tired eyes. "Thank you, David."

"I mean, he was a genius."

"Yes," sherry agreed, "He was very intelligent."

The van motor purred hypnotically as they swiftly passed under overpasses and lighted directories.

"You and Mr. Moore didn't never have no children, did you?"

Sherry didn't answer. She would have liked children, but she knew she could never give Ben any.

"I'm sorry Ma'am. That's none of my business. I was just thinking that I never delivered diapers to your place. I didn't mean nothing by it."

"No offense taken, David." Sherry closed her eyes again. She couldn't tell for how long, but soon, she felt the ground change under the van's tires. The vehicle was pitching and bumping again. She should be home any minute. Then she remembered the $20. Sherry forced her eyes open and searched around for her purse. It was by the driver's seat. As she leaned forward to reach for the purse, the van moved onto a gravel road.

"David? I don't recognize this road."

"I'm sorry, Ma'am, I missed the turn. I can cut across here and not lose any time."

Sherry grabbed her purse and stood up with difficulty, trying to maintain her balance. Upright, she could now see out through the front windshield. They were off the road, heading into the woods. She turned toward David to ask him about it when the vehicle suddenly jerked forward. The purse spilled as she propelled back toward the rear of the van. The vehicle screeched to a stop. She tried to get up. But David was instantly on top of her.

"David! What are you doing?"

David pinned her on the van floor. She struggled to push him off but he grabbed her arm and pressed it tightly against her. Sitting on top of her, he produced a shiny, stainless steel, barber's razor. He pressed it to her throat.

"Ain't no use in fighting, Ma'am. It'll only make things worse."

Sherry tried to squirm under his weight but he was too strong. She grabbed his right hand that held the blade to her throat, but she couldn't move it away. She tried to pull her other arm free but it was under his knee. It was no use. How could she have been so stupid? How could she not have been more cautious? Now she was helpless to prevent what would happen. Her pretty jacket was torn, and her skirt was bunched up above her thighs. Sherry began to cry.

"Don't cry!"

Sherry struggled to stop crying.

"I don't like it when you cry," demanded David with a shove.

"Why.... Why me?"

"You? A young widow and all. I'll bet it's been a long time since you been with a man."

"David . . . don't."

"Why not? I bet you'll even like it."

"David.... You need help. I could get you help. Sometimes I work at the hospital and—"

"Shut up! I don't wanna hear that! Shut up!" he shouted. Shaking her with each command.

Sherry could see his wide staring eyes in the darkness. She tried to say something but stopped.

"I tell you what I wanna hear. Tell me you love me. Yea, that's it. Tell me you love me. And if you prove it to me . . . I'll let you go."

Sherry tried to squirm free again, but David bore down harder. She wished she had been home by now. She knew this would be her end. It would be all over for her. If only she could have been home before midnight. He moved the razor down from her throat to her stomach and began cutting the buttons off her jacket. She tried to pull her right arm free as she felt him cut the buttons off her blouse.

"David," she whimpered.

"Tell me you love me or don't say nothin!"

Sherry began to feel sick. She seize his razor arm, driving her nails into his wrist. Her thoughts began to blur. A flush of heat began to spread over her torso as her watch chimed the turn of the hour and the dial indicated midnight. Her body trembled under David. He moved her arm from her chest. The cold metal blade slipped under the center of her bra, easily cutting the garment free. She began to shake violently . . . and a deep guttural sound filled the van.

Sherry's arm twisted free to claw at David's face. He tried to push it away from his face with his blade hand as Sherry wriggled free of her jacket. Suddenly she had claws. Enormous front claws that savagely gouged, cleaved, and shred David's chest—hind claws that ripped his lower torso, and fangs that tore his throat. He slashed at her with his razor but a stainless steel blade was of little use. David needed silver to stop this newly formed creature. Pounding thuds rocked the van as growls and screams echoed in the darkness.

Coherent thought rapidly faded in Sherry's mind. Now, only instinctively, did she know that she would have to relocate. She would have to move the lair. It would be sunrise before she could think rationally again. Sunrise before she would regret not having reached home before midnight. And, it would be noon before she would be capable of feeling guilt. Right now, she only felt hunger. A ravenous unrelenting hunger that could only be satisfied by feeding on raw flesh.

Rest in Piece
By
Glenda Mills

Here lies dearly departed Fred
His head lay quietly on his bed
The footboard cradled both his feet
His body rested on the sheet
His arms hung limply in defeat
His throat was cut from ear to ear
We buried all the pieces here

The Man Under the Bed

by

Jeannine Baumgartle

The first time it had happened, Gordon remembered, there was no other word for it but adorable, his son in his bear pajamas, wanting to climb him like a tree, not even crying out, just clinging like he was scared to death.

"What is it, Mick?" he'd asked him, more than once, trying to get him to say what the problem was, the small flushed face turning from side to side, trying to get away even from his questions.

"In there." His arm pointed toward his bedroom, then drew back into safety.

"What's in there, Mick?" Gordon pulled away enough for eye-contact. Reasonable, was the approach he would like Mick to adopt.

"A monster," Mick informed him as though he hadn't been paying attention.

"It's alright, son. We'll go shoo him out."

"No, no! Stay here! Gord found himself caught up in the urgency of his son's cries, and sheltered him with his body under the covers.

"Ah, what's this?" Shelley said, easing in next to them. "A small visitor?" She rolled her round tummy toward them. Mick was still tense.

"Nightmare," Gord explained.

"Uumm." She did mother things, then, that comforted both of them, words, touches, assurances. Gordon did not want her always having to do this. With another baby coming, she really needed her sleep.

Next morning, Mick was up and bouncing cheerfully off the walls.

When the monster came again, Gordon turned on lights and checked under the bed, and in all the closet drawers. The tucking-in ritual followed, but Mick was in their room again in seconds, his fears as real as his trembling. They hauled him in with them, and when he had gone to sleep, carried him back to his own room.

The next night, Gord waited for the monster to call, and when it did, he swept his son up and hustled him out, so Shelley could sleep.

They looked all through the room again and went through the tucking-in, but Mick wouldn't let him go. Gord had visions of having to sleep in his son's bed every night, and hastily regrouped.

"Tell you what, Mick." Daddy's going to stay *under* the bed tonight. "I'm too big for anything else to get under there. What do you think?" It was also a lot easier to sneak out without being missed.

Mick, holding up a section of bedspread, watched him shimmy under the frame. It was carpeted under the bed, and a rather tight fit. His nose touched the gauzy weave of the fabric tacked onto the bottom of the box springs. A slat or two fenced him into claustrophobic immobility, his feet outside the spread's overhang.

"Now, can anything else *fit* under here?"

His son stared at him with his blue eyes and shook his head.

"Okay, then. Run turn off the lights, and go to sleep."

Little feet padded obediently away from him. Mick managed the light switch, than ran and jumped onto the bed, wriggling quickly under the covers.

"All right up there?" Gord asked, not too sure *he* was, after that unexpected impact.

"Daddy?"

"Yes?"

"Are you there?"

"Yes."

"Is it just you?"

"Uh, Mick, if anything else were here, I'd know it."

Mick settled down after that, and quiet eventually took over the house.

Lying there, Gord waited to hear the easy breathing that meant his son had relaxed and fallen asleep. But it was as if Mick was holding

his breath, too. It really was dark under the bed. He was suddenly aware of not having a pillow, and of coolness at his feet. If he moved, adjusted in any way, he would disturb Mick. Poor little Mick, cowering above him, wishing for a real person next to him, not hidden away somewhere.

This may not have been the best way to handle the problem. It wouldn't work for either of them. Mick wouldn't sleep, and he wouldn't be able to get away. He thought back, trying to remember how his parents had coped with things like this. He was pretty sure he remembered his Dad, with a light, the doorway behind him, to the right, the corner of the room with all his things piled there, that old sled, rusting away, the khaki pup-tent with its strings and stakes, the clothes his mom had asked him to pick up...

Suddenly he realized the light was on, his son pulling at his pants leg. He shut his mouth, a post-snoring motion, and realized he'd probably fallen asleep.

"Dad. Time your bed," Mick said.

Gordon groped his way out of the side of his packaging. "Did we get the monsters, buddy?"

Mick nodded, as though placating him, gave him a desultory hug and plopped himself back onto his bed.

He wasn't summoned again.

The Lost Souls

by
Joy Kirchgessner

The dream came again. I hadn't had it since I'd moved to Boston. But every time that I returned to Ridgeport, Kentucky for a visit it would happen all over again. I'm walking barefoot, lost in a dense forest on a moonlit night. The ground is covered with a thick fog, and the brambles tear at my skin. I have a feeling of overwhelming despair. Then, surrounding me, many headstones appear, intermingled among the trunks of the trees. At each headstone the tree roots swell up through the fog like giant cypress knees, then they turn into ghostly forms of men, women, and children, rising from these lonesome graves. The ghosts glide slowly towards me with arms outstretched, palms, upward. I know they are trying to say something. I don't want to hear it and cup my hands over my ears. A dark figure, a silhouette appears between the ghosts and me. This figure is more ominous than the ghosts are. Every one of my muscles is frozen in panic. I try to scream but I can't make a sound. The intensity of the hysterics jolts me out of the nightmare. I awake sitting straight up in my bed, and by the soft morning light, I quickly take in the comforting familiarity of my room and reassure myself that it was only a dream.

I was staying with my close friend, Diane. We had been friends since childhood. When she married and moved to Ridgeport I came to visit whenever I got the chance. We took long walks on the hiking paths in the state forest that framed the grassy fields of her farm and chatted about old times and new. We both enjoyed the outdoors. For the past few years the phone and email were as close to visiting as we could get. Business had kept me away; it wasn't easy starting an art gallery. But this visit had a much more solemn itinerary. Her husband, Glen, had died in a boating accident on Celina Lake, a lake that was in the same state forest that we loved to hike through. She found him face down in the water on the shoreline near his boat. As far as the police and the coroner could tell, he had fallen and hit his head on a large rock while trying to pull his small fishing boat up on a slick bank. The lake wasn't far behind their farm: approximately three-quarters of a mile and bordered on three sides by state forest. It was a favorite fishing spot of Glen's.

I booked a two o'clock flight to the Louisville, Kentucky airport and rented a car; I intended to stay for a couple of weeks. My manager had assured me he could handle the gallery. It would take three hours to drive to Diane's farm. As I drove I thought about what she had told me about her husband's death. Glen had taken their dog, Brownie,

with him to the lake. Her dog had come home alone and with a large gash on its shoulder that later had to be stitched. She had then driven up to the lake. She spotted her husband's empty boat near the shore on the far side of the lake, the one part that was privately owned. Glen never pulled the boat in there. She had to run all the way around the lake in order to get to the other side. The closer she got the more she felt that something was terribly wrong. And then when she saw his body half in, half out of the water.... I shuddered off the thought.

When I arrived at Diane's farm she was sitting on the front porch, her big chocolate lab, Brownie, at her feet with his head between his paws. Her parents were in the house. Not wanting to leave Diane alone, they had been waiting for me. We unloaded my suitcases and put them in the spare room. I comforted her the best I could by letting her tell the sad story again. Exhausted, we finally went to our beds around midnight. The funeral was in the morning. Tomorrow would be a long painful day.

I had a dream, but this time it was about Glen. He got up out of his grave, walked up to the house, and knocked on the front door. I awoke to the sound of Diane knocking on my bedroom door telling me she had coffee and breakfast ready.

Diane and I entered the Leamann Funeral Home. I can say that a funeral home is not one of my most favorite places and if I had my choice I would only enter if I were the one in the casket, but there are some things in life that must be done. The funeral home director met us at the door. He was dressed in the obligatory dark suit and bore a smile. He had a look that made me feel like he was taking measurements for the next coffin. Diane introduced me. His name was Robert Leamann, owner of the funeral home. He was a tall thin man with hollow cheeks and deep-set eyes. His hair was black and it made his face look sallow. He reached out with bony fingers to shake my hand. I limply held out my hand in return but only let my fingers touch his in half-gesture. I felt like I was shaking hands with Death himself.

As we walked away Diane told me that Mr. Leamann was the county coroner. He also owned the property where Glen was found. She felt sorry for Mr. Leamann, for he had told her that he somehow felt responsible just because he owned that piece of property.

Glen's wish was to be cremated and his ashes scattered on the lake. I had never been to a funeral where this was to be the procedure. The funeral was held as normal but then the body was taken away afterwards. In a couple of days the ashes would be returned to Diane.

Early the next morning, Diane needed to go into town to the lawyer and take care of some type of paperwork. Her parents and Glen's were going with her. I told her I would stay at the house and maybe go for a little walk on one of our favorite paths in the woods. I wouldn't go too far, I just wanted to make a few sketches to take back with me.

The sun was just rising as I picked up my sketch pad and a couple of pencils and headed across the field for the trees that bordered her property. Brownie was in his pen and protested my leaving him behind but I didn't want to have to watch after him. The morning sun felt good on my shoulders as I walked through the field full of yellow Black-

Eyed-Susans and orange Butterfly Weeds. I sat down beneath the shade of a grand old oak tree at the edge of the forest and leaned back against the trunk. For a few minutes I looked up and watched the hypnotizing play of light through the leaves and tried to clear my mind. Then I picked up my sketch pad to draw the flowers of the Butterfly Weed full of fluttering wings. But there was something else there, too. Droplets of a dark shade of red on the bright orange blossoms. I bent nearer and the butterflies scattered, brushing their delicate wings against my face. It was blood and there were larger droplets on the leaves on a path beside me leading into the forest. I got up to have a better look. There were cloven tracks on the path, which I recognized as deer. I'd seen the blood pattern before. More than likely it was from a wounded deer. It could run for quite a distance on an adrenaline rush. I walked several feet into the woods and searched for more signs of the blood. The deer must have gotten off of the path. I turned around and there beside the path was a pile of red and purple intestines, a few hours old and still moist.

"Isn't it a shame?" came a voice from behind me.

I jumped sideways and nearly tripped on a root. For a moment I was blinded because of the rising sun and all I could see was a silhouette of whoever had spoken. It brought back the memory of my haunting dream and sent a chill down my spine. Then Robert Leamann stepped out of the light. He was dressed in black sweats.

"I'm sorry, did I startle you?" he said. "I'm Robert Leamann. I believe you're... Diane's friend?"

I nodded and kept my distance.

His gaze turned to the pile of intestines as he walked over to them. "Hard to tell that this was once a magnificent animal. Must have been a poacher. I found this arrow over there." He pointed to the opposite side of the path.

But I watched the arrow. It had a green plastic shaft and a razor sharp triangular metal point. With the arrow he prodded and turned the pile. Then he pointed at two vein ridden yellowish sacs. "You can see what strong lungs it had. In a few days you won't even be able to tell that much. It's a shame. Ashes to ashes, dust to dust."

Then he looked at me and said, "I often walk these woods. Nature lover I guess. Relieves the tensions of the day. I suppose that's why you're out here, too?"

My heart was still pounding and my hair felt like it was standing on end. I answered, nodding my head before any sound came out. "Yes." One word is all I could say.

He continued, "Maybe it's not safe to be out here in the woods just now. I'd estimate that what's left of this poor animal is not but a few hours old. Is Diane with you?"

"No, she had to go to town. She's probably home waiting for me by now. Nice talking to you but I'd better get back and meet her." I was walking backwards and away as I said this and then turned and ran all the way back to the house.

I told Diane about the encounter with Mr. Leamann. She said maybe he had been in the business much too long. And he does take long walks in the woods so it wouldn't be unusual to meet up with him.

I didn't want to worry her so I dropped the subject.

After a few days Mr. Leamann gave Diane a small urn that contained Glen's ashes. Diane and I drove up to the lake; Brownie was in the back seat, his head hanging out the window. Both sets of parents followed in their own cars. We left Brownie in the car and got into Glen's small fishing boat. I rowed her out to the center and with a silent prayer she sprinkled his ashes across the water.

Brownie was barking and had wriggled out of the car window. The parents couldn't catch him and he ran the long path around the lake and to the other side. He stood there on the bank and barked at us. He was accustomed to riding in the boat with Glen. Then he turned and disappeared into the dense woods on Mr. Leamann's property.

"Oh cute, we have to row over and get him," said Diane. "I don't want to leave him up here. He's probably already pulled the stitches in his shoulder loose."

We rowed over to the spot where Glen had been found. Mr. Leamann had since posted No Trespassing signs on almost every tree lining his side of the lake. We both got out and pulled the boat onto the shore. We walked into the woods and started calling for Brownie. With a thrashing of leaves he came bounding through the underbrush towards us, but there was something in his mouth. I recognized what it was and screamed, "Oh, God, Diane *run!*"

"But wha—" she uttered.

I grabbed her hand and with me half-dragging her, we ran for the boat. We pushed the boat off of the gritty bank and into the water and jumped in. I grasped both oars and rowed with a fury.

"What about Brownie?" she wailed.

"Brownie can meet us on the other side of the lake."

Brownie, now on the bank, bounded into the water but stopped when he was in but a few inches, looking stunned that we left him behind. A human arm dangled from his jaws.

The next day the paper read:

> Ridgeport, Ky. - So far 53 bodies have been unearthed on private property owned by Robert Leamann, Brent County coroner and owner of Leamann Funeral Home. Corpses were also found in the basement of Mr. Leamann's home. It has been alleged that he was performing bizarre experiments in the belief that he could raise the dead. Investigators refuse to speculate how many bodies will be found or comment on how the people died.
>
> Mr. Robert Leamann has been arrested on suspicion of murder. Law enforcement officials are investigating the death a of local resident, Glen Bowers. Mr. Bowers was a neighbor of Robert Leamann.

The People From Down Below

by
Marian Allen

They come out after dark.
The planks beneath my bed rattle and hiss
then the shadows crawl out,
draw each other out,
stifling groans,
smelling like dirt and bodies.

"How'd you sleep?" Momma asks
in the morning light.
"Fine," I say. She nods.
"Your daddy's gone
with the buckboard," she says,
"with a load of corn to the station."

"Sleep all right?" Daddy asks
another day.
"Yes, sir," I say,
remembering the writhing forms
painting dark on dark against my floor,
shadow creeping up the doorframe
lifting the latch
easing out.
"Couple of Momma's cousins come over from Vincennes,"
he says. "She's taking them to visit Aunt Cora."

I crawl beneath my bed and scratch
a cross on each board. I scratch
a cross on my door, and on the walls
and on the window frame.
If I can't keep them under the bed
I'll keep them with me,
away from Momma and Daddy,
keep my people safe.

Still they come.
Still they go.

Then, one day,
I whisper. In the barn,
me and Daddy and Stella
the red cow. I tell him
and I ask.

"They're just passing through,"
he says. "Forget them in the morning.
They come from Hell,
bound for the Promised Land.
Pray for them, baby. Pray."

The New Kid
by
Mary Gehant-Lagunez

"Hey, Jack, hurry up! Aren't you ready yet?" Gene Garvey yelled up the stairwell. She was on time, as usual.

Jack grabbed his jacket, a notebook and pencil and thundered down the stairs in time to hear his Aunt Bess tell Mrs. Garvey that she "would be delighted to have Regina here today, Dorothy."

"I hate these Saturday meetings; did they have them when you were still teaching, Mrs. Simonton? But I must run—we start at 9:30," Mrs. Garvey was saying.

Aunt Bess chuckled. "Oh my, yes. Conferences always seemed to come up at the worst times. As if teachers ever have much free time during the school year, anyway." She then turned to Jack. "Are you two going to study together this morning?"

"Nuh...not exactly. We're going to go over to the woods near the old Barlow place. We've got to write some kind of dopey thing about spring for English, so we thought we'd see if anything's happening—if the pond ice has broken up or something—maybe there's plants coming up. I dunno. What's for lunch?"

"Vegetable soup and cheese sandwiches; I think there's enough soup left over for the three of us. Are you dressed warmly? Do be careful near the pond, now. This early, you never know what's underfoot. And the ground is so muddy and slippery you could fall into a puddle and catch your death of cold before you could get back home. Do you have a watch with you? Be back by noon—you'll both have to clean up before sitting down to the table." Aunt Bess usually had lots of advice for her youngest nephew.

Jack assured her that yes, they'd be careful, did have enough on and would be on time for lunch. He gave her a quick, trying-to-be-a-tough-guy hug and headed to the front door. Gene was already out, waving goodbye to her mother.

"Honestly, I still don't see why I couldn't have stayed home," Gene said. "I'm almost 13 now, and loads of kids are home alone all the time."

"Yeah, I hear you. Aunt Bess is the same way. She says since we're out in the country here, no telling who's around or what could happen, and she 'just couldn't face your parents if you were hurt while you're staying with me.' As if it would."

The two youngsters turned down the road, crossing over to walk against the traffic. Not that much traffic came along their road, which connected two county secondaries. Its main purpose was to serve the dozen farms along a 12-mile stretch.

"Umm, smell the mud," Gene said. "Dad always says that when he can first smell wet ground as the snow melts, he knows spring is coming. Write that down—about smelling it, not about Dad."

Jack dutifully noted that they could smell wet mud.

"And look how much water's in the ditch. It's almost like a stream," Gene added.

"Isn't there always water in the ditch?" Jack asked.

"Not always. But now, with all the run-off from snow, there's a ton of it. Wasn't there lots of water around during the spring, back in Chicago?"

"Never noticed," Jack replied. "The streets were always plowed, and any water went into the sewers." Again, he scribbled a note that the ditch was full of water.

Jack Hughes had moved to his aunt's home in southern Wisconsin the fall before. His grandmother had had a stroke at the end of August, just after his father received word that he'd be shuttling between Chicago and a new plant which his firm was opening up in Mexico. That meant that his parents were in no position to manage a household.

"What have you heard from your folks?" Gene asked.

"Got a couple of E-mails this week. Gram is doing a lot better—she's home, but is still going to rehab every day, so Mom has to take her, stay with her and then bring her home. Plus everything else. Dad's in Mexico now, but he's coming home next week and they say they're coming up here for a visit. I sure hope so." The youngsters walked on.

Less than a mile from Aunt Bess' driveway the two came to the place where a farmer had made a path for his vehicles to enter fields. They opened the gate and started along the lane—really two tracks which were, this early in spring, two trickles of water over mud. They picked their way along the ridge between the ruts.

At the far end of the field, the fence sagged where hunters and fishermen had climbed through it to enter the woods adjacent to the farm. Jack stood on one strand of barbed wire and pulled the other up, helping Gene through. Then she returned the favor for him.

"Where is Barlow, anyhow?" Jack asked. "Aunt Bess says that farm is empty."

"Mr. Barlow was really old when he died last year," Gene answered. "I think I heard Dad say a cousin inherited it and maybe is going to sell it to someone who wants to cut the woods and grow vegetables on it, on a contract with the canning factory over in Smithton. How gross. It's just a really neat place, with the trees and the pond and everything. Oh, look - there's a purple finch. I haven't seen one since last fall."

"Where? I don't see any purple bird."

"There, under that bush. And there's another one, too."

"They look like sparrows to me." Jack was a city boy, after all.

"They're the same size, and they've got stripes, but can't you see the red around their heads?"

"Oh, yeah, I guess so. They still look like sparrows. Why are they called purple, when they're not?"

"How do I know? But write down that we saw purple finches. They're not around in winter, so it's another sign of spring."

Jack made another note.

The path leading to the pond was just a trail. At this time of year, the footing was uncertain, with half-rotted leaves over the ground. Both youngsters slipped from time to time as they walked. Gene pointed out buds forming on the trees, or new growth peeking up through the soil. Jack carefully entered everything in his notebook.

A slight rise of ground led them deeper into the woods and away from the farmland. Suddenly Gene, who was walking first, stopped. "I think someone's up ahead of us. Do you see anything?" she asked.

"I don't know...who could it be?" Jack replied. He tried to look through the bare branches, but the second-growth trees grew close to-gether, and a fair number of evergreens blocked a clear view of the path in front of them.

"If it's Peterson and Schmitt, we're in for it. They're the only other kids who live around here. Anyone else, it's okay," she answered.

"I think I see him…only one person. I don't think it's either Peterson or Schmitt, and anyway, they always stick together."

"Yeah, either of them is a pain, and the two of them…well, it's worse than double trouble," Gene said. "They can't seem to think of anything else but picking on smaller kids."

She peered along the path as they moved forward cautiously. "I think it's a kid—not tall enough to be an adult."

The figure in front of them paused and looked back towards them. He (or could it be a girl?) had long hair caught behind his back and was wearing a rather long, belted jacket and knee boots. As Gene and Jack walked on, he seemed to melt into the woods by the path.

They were puzzled by how quickly the other person had stepped out of view, but whoever it was, he looked okay.

In any event, they had to pick their way carefully. A dip in the path was covered by a small stream which normally flowed through a pipe, but was now carrying far too much water to remain in its bed. While the water was only an inch deep on the path, it formed sizeable pools on both sides of it.

Gene and Jack picked their way across carefully. "If we slip, we'll be soaked," Jack said. "Hang on... let's only one of us move at a time. Just how deep is that water, anyway?"

"Only a foot or so—but I sure don't want to step into it." They held hands, steadying each other as they crossed.

Rounding a curve, they saw the other boy again, this time about 20 yards ahead. "Hi—you new around here?" Gene called.

"Noooo…are you Jack Hughes?" the other boy was looking intently at Jack. He seemed to be about their age.

"Yeah—how do you know my name?" asked Jack. He'd never seen the kid before, and now they could see that his clothes definitely hadn't come from Wal-Mart.

"Wow, that's a neat jacket," Gene stared at the soft leather. "It looks like deerskin…where'd you get it?"

"My mother made it for me."

"You know my name—what's yours?" Jack was puzzled and a bit irritated that his question hadn't been answered.

"You can call me… Fox," was the reply.

"I've never seen you in school," Gene, too, was puzzled. "Where do you live? What school do you go to?"

Fox waved vaguely in the direction of the pond. "I don't go...to school. My uncles tell me what I need to know."

"Oh, home-schooled. But how do you know me?" Jack was still irked that Fox recognized him, but he had never seen Fox before.

"My people have known your family for a long time. I thought it must be you, but I wanted to know," Fox answered. "Why haven't I've seen you before?" So far, he had been watching Jack and scarcely noticing Gene. That was beginning to get to her. After all, *she* had been living here right along, not Jack.

"I came up to stay with my Aunt B...well, really, Dad's Aunt Bess...last fall. But I've never heard them talking about any old friends around here. When did our folks meet?" Jack was still wondering about that.

"Long ago." Fox shifted his gaze from Jack back to the path they'd been on. "Someone else is coming. Two – oh, I've seen them before. They are not friends to the woods. I don't like them. Do you know them?"

Gene and Jack looked back. It was Peterson and Schmitt. On their bikes, too.

"They're idiots, trying to ride bikes up here when it's so muddy. But if they see us, they'll try to beat us up or something." Gene tried not to show that she was scared.

"They're not your friends? Good. Come – I know where you can hide so they won't see you." Fox moved quietly forward, stepped off the path and through a group of firs. There was a faint trail which Gene and Jack followed. "Here, behind this log. I'll take care of them."

"Be careful, Fox," said Gene. "There's two of them, and they're pretty strong. They'll try to beat you up."

"They won't see me. Watch where the creek crosses the path." Fox motioned them forward, then slipped back to the path and ran lightly towards the little stream.

"How can he get rid of Peterson and Schmitt all by himself?" Gene wondered. "And how can he run like that? We were sliding all over the place coming up."

"I dunno. But he seems to know what he's doing. Geez. Look at

those dweebs—they're trying to *ride* over that creek. Where's Fox?"

Peterson was leading the way, with Schmitt on his tail. Just as Peterson was almost across the creek, his front wheel twisted and he fell right into the pond on one side of the path. Schmitt braked, his bike slid out from under him and he bellyflopped, into the water on the other side. Both howled.

The two kids pulled themselves up, still standing in the water. They were soaking wet and muddy. Schmitt shouted something—Gene and Jack couldn't make out what—at Peterson.

Doubling over, hands clasped over their mouths to keep from laughing out loud, Gene and Jack watched as Peterson pulled himself out of the water and righted his bike. They couldn't hear what he was saying, but Schmidt didn't seem to like it. Then—could it really be?—Peterson punched Schmidt!

The two bullies pulled their bikes back on the path and headed home, still arguing.

Suddenly, both kids were startled by Fox, who slipped out of nearby trees. "They're gone. They didn't like the water." For the first time, Fox let himself grin a bit. "They are bad. They break branches for no reason, throw stones at birds. I am glad that you don't like them either."

He turned and started walking up the path.

"Hey—are you coming back here again?" Jack called after him. A sudden wish to talk more with Fox, to learn more about their families' friendship, arose in Jack's mind.

By now Fox was quite far ahead of them. He stopped for a moment, and said, "Yes, I think so. I don't know when." He took a few more steps, turned back and raised one hand in farewell.

And disappeared.

There's Something Evil in the Deep Dark Woods
By
Elizabeth J. Gross

Some people know the exact moment their lives change – things, that just an instant before were important, become obsolete. A paradigm shift. "If only I had done this, or not done that," they might ask themselves, "would things have turned out differently? Would I be richer, poorer, healthier or sicker or, perhaps, somebody could have lived and not died?" Sherry's chaotic life was a constant change, but if someone were to ask Rachel what catastrophic thing altered her life, she would answer, "When I picked up the phone."

Rachel, carrying a Sunday morning newspaper and breakfast tray, was on her way back to bed when the phone rang. "Damn," she said, pausing to look at the Caller I.D. *Sherry Tate*. Letting the answering machine take it, she heard her own voice say, "Leave a message." Then, "Rachel! Rachel! Pick up! If you're there, pick up!" Knowing if she didn't answer, Sherry would keep calling, she yanked the phone from its cradle.

"What?" she demanded.

"Well, good afternoon to you, too. Did we sleep on a nail last night?"

"Yeah, well, I guess so. Just taking life's frustrations out on you. Sorry. What's up?"

"Wanna take a ride with me? I have to go up in the mountains to the cabin. Jason needs some papers he left up there last weekend. I have to FAX them to him in San Francisco. I don't want to go up there by myself. Too scary."

"No," Rachel said, eyeing the bed. It looked warm and inviting – offering a long, lazy afternoon with her breakfast and the newspaper; a nap, and then to the studio for that interview with Senator Ramsey.

"Come on, Rachel. What else have you got going? Taking a nap? Look, you need to get out. Have a social life. You're either at the studio or in the bed – by yourself. What kind of life is that?"

"Can't. Got things to do and I have to be at the station by eight. I'm taping an interview with Ramsey for the eleven o'clock news. You know that. I told you yesterday."

"It won't take all afternoon to go up to the cabin. We'll be back in plenty of time before eight."

"I don't know…" The bed looked sooo inviting, but she had to ask, "When are you leaving?"

"Get dressed! I'm leaving now! Be there in fifteen minutes!" Click.

"Damn! I can't believe I asked! Well, maybe it won't be so bad. A ride up in the Appalachians might clear my brain," she said, pulling jeans and a flannel shirt out of her closet. She was making a sandwich out of her bacon and eggs when Sherry blew the car horn. Grabbing a lightweight jacket, Rachel went out the door. It wasn't too cold for October, she thought, and she mostly would be in the car.

"What're you eating?" Sherry asked, as Rachel closed the car door.

"My breakfast."

"It's two o'clock!"

Rachel gave her a look. "Listen up now. I have to be back home by six. Noooo later, Sherry! I have to shower, dress and get to the TV station by eight."

"I know! I know! We'll make it! We'll get to the cabin by three, I'll get the papers, we'll leave, go to a little restaurant, eat, and be back here by six sharp. No sweat. No foolin'." She grinned.

"Okay. I'm holding you to it."

"Rrrready, Roy?" Sherry asked in her best Gabby Hayes imitation.

Rachel laughed. "Yuuup."

Sherry left rubber tracks on the pavement when she peeled out of the driveway.

As the Jeep began its ascent into the mountains, they rode in silence for a while, enjoying the colorful display of the red and gold leaves.

"You know, that's all it has done for a month. Rain," Sherry said, turning on the wipers.

"I heard from Jeff," Rachel said.

"Oh, yeah? When?"

"Yesterday. He wants me to file for divorce. She's pregnant… and they want to get married."

"Oh, geez, Rachel, I'm sorry. Does it hurt—really bad?"

"No, not as much as it did. You know," Rachel said, changing the subject, "fall is my favorite time of the year. The trees are beautiful and the sound of the rain makes it nice and cozy in here." She smiled at Sherry. "I'm really glad I came. I've lived here nearly five years, but I haven't been far up in these mountains. Have you?"

Taking the hint, Sherry said, "Nope. No farther than the cabin. It's quite a ways up there, and it gets really wild back in the bush. I wouldn't want to be caught in there at night without a big strongman with a big strong gun. When we stayed up there, we heard wolves howling a lot. That puts a shiver right down your spine. Don't worry," she said when she saw Rachel's look, "we'll be outta here before dark. It's a little after three now. Get that piece of paper out of my purse. I drew a map on it. It tells me how to get to the cabin."

"*A map!* Don't you know how to get to the cabin?"

"Well, sorta. I never drove it before. I just rode. I looked at the scenery, not the route. We should be turning up here soon, I think."

After rummaging around in Sherry's oversized purse, Rachel said, "There's no map in here."

"Sure there is…cripes! I left it on the table! But nnnnnever ya' mind, Roy, Ol' Hannbal'll get us home."

Rachel laughed. "That wasn't Gabby's horse's name, was it?"

"Heck, who knows. I think this is it,' she said, making a turn on an unpaved side road.

"You sure?"

"Sure as rain." She laughed. "Now, we stay on this little road for a while, then we turn again. Look for a big ol' rock on your right. That's where we turn…I think."

"*You think!* God, Sherry, don't you really know? Don't do this! You're scaring me!" Rachel said, looking around at the thick growth of trees, weeds and bushes. "We could get lost in here! Who knows we came up here, anyway?"

"Jason."

"But you said he was in San Francisco. Who knows around here?"

"Well, nearly nobody. I told Bowzer."

"*The dog? You only* told your *dog?*"

"Don't worry. Everything's fine. He's a Saint Bernard. Here's where we turn, I think."

"I don't see the big rock."

"Maybe I was wrong. I believe it's farther on down this road here." She made a turn on a more dismal, narrow and scarier road than before.

"Sherry, I don't believe anyone has used this road for a long, long time. I don't even think it's a road. It's more like a path—*an animal path!*"

They bumped along for a while, made a few more turns, then Sherry stopped the Jeep. "Right or left. Your call."

"*My call?* God, Sherry! Let's go back! I don't like this! This isn't a road anymore! Nothing human has been along here in a while—if ever!" Rachel shivered. "It's getting late, too! We've been wandering around in here forever!"

It began to rain hard. Sherry backed up, and pulled forward, then backed up again.

"*Be careful!* You don't know what's in back of you! We could go over a cliff!"

"*I'm being careful!*" The Jeep's wheels spun, then caught and they crept forward. "Look at that rain come down!" Then, suddenly, something huge and black sprang out of the bushes and ran across in front of them. "*God!*" Sherry shrieked, slamming on the brakes. "Did you see that? What was it?"

"I don't know! I've never seen anything like it!"

"Was it a bear?"

"No, I don't think it was a bear. I couldn't see too good for the rain, but it looked like it had wings on its back."

"*Then, Rachel, it wasn't a bear! Bears don't have wings!*" Sherry screeched.

"I didn't say it was! *You* asked if it was a bear."

The wind grew fierce, bending trees and slamming hard rain against the automobile. Thunder rolled and lightning streaked across the sky. "*Let's get outta here!*" Sherry yelled, stomping on the accelerator. The Jeep lurched forward, then sideways and slipped down a steep hill. The car tilted, rolled over on its top and wedged against a tree. Dangling upside down, the women were held in place by their seatbelts.

"God, Sherry! Look what you've done!"

"I couldn't help it! The car slid!" she yelled back.

"I smell gasoline," Rachel said, coughing. "Something must have ruptured the gas tank." A loud boom of thunder pealed overhead, and, *powwww!* lightning hit a tree just a few yards from the Jeep.

"We're going to get hit by lightning and burn to death!" Sherry screamed, jerking frantically at the seatbelt. *"Omigod! Help me! This seatbelt won't work!"*

Rachel hit the release button and fell onto the roof. "Be still, Sherry! I'm going to get you out. Quit struggling! Here goes!" *Whump!* Sherry, with a grunt, landed on the car top.

Rachel kicked at her car door, then crawled to the back doors and kicked them. Rivulets of raw gasoline were streaming into the car, making it difficult to breathe. "Try your door, Sherry," she choked out. "Kick it!" Nothing. All the doors were stuck and the windows were intact. "God! I hate automatic windows!" She needed something to break the glass. *Blam!* Thunder clapped directly overhead, rolling through the wind-torn, rain-deluged mountains. Reaching up and feeling around under the seat, her fingers closed on a wrench.

Sherry was rummaging around in her purse. "Rachel," she coughed, "do you have your cell phone?"

Rachel, ready to whack the glass with the wrench, turned and asked, "No, why? A cell phone? Oh, God! We don't have one, do we?"

"I left it at home on the table… with the map!" Sherry wailed.

Seriously fighting the urge to hit Sherry with the wrench, Rachel struck the pane, cracking it. She hit it again, and chunks of safety glass fell from the window frame. As Rachel beat the remaining glass out with the wrench, a streak of lightning hit close to the Jeep. *"Get out, Sherry! If lightning hits us, we'll burn alive!"* she rasped through a gasoline-raw throat, and pulled herself out the window.

"I can't, Rachel!" she choked, **"That thing's out there!"**

"Then stay, Sherry!" Rachel's hoarse voice was nearly lost in the wind. "It'll be a toss-up what gets you first! The *thing* or the lightning!" And she left, putting distance between her and the Jeep fire-bomb.

Seeing her friend leaving and terrified of being alone, Sherry climbed out of the vehicle and hurried after her.

Quickly choosing the hill over a nearly impenetrable thicket, they struggled upward a few feet, when, suddenly a big stick came hurling through the air. It glanced off Rachel's arm, knocking her down the slippery bank. Dazed, she heard Sherry shrieking.

"Oh, God! Rachel! It's that thing! It's coming down after us! Run!" Sherry cried, loping down the hill. *"Get up, Rachel! Run!"*

Looking up, Rachel saw a huge, wolf-like animal making its way down. Pulling herself up, she chased Sherry back past the Jeep and into the dense underbrush.

Knowing the animal was coming, they thrashed blindly through the brambles. Suddenly, coming out of the bushes, they nearly fell into a wide creek.

"It's coming, Rachel! What'll we do? I can't swim! Oh, God! Oh, God! Oh, God!"

"Sherry, please shut up! Just shut up!" Rachel demanded, grabbing her friend's arm and pulling her along the creek bank. It was almost five o'clock, and the storm was quickly bringing darkness to the woods. Mercifully, the rain had lessened, and the storm seemed to have moved on.

The upper part of the creek was rain-swollen. What had been a waterfall, was now blocked by debris with only trickles of water going over the side. About thirty or forty feet below, the water was shallow, with a wide sandbar sticking up in the middle. A good-sized tree lay across the dammed-up waterfall, reaching from one bank to the other. Rachel climbed up on the tree, dragging Sherry after her and they began to inch their way across. They were over the middle of the creek, when, suddenly, the end of the tree lifted in back of them. It was violently twisted to the left, throwing Sherry down into the swollen stream. Rachel managed to hold on to a limb. Then the tree was roughly twisted to the right and pitched over the waterfall. Rachel hit the sandbar flat on her back. The tree landed across her hips, pinning her.

Sherry, spluttering, held on to a log and kicked toward the shore. A terrible pain in her side made it difficult to climb out of the water. After struggling up the bank, she saw a piece of wood jutting through her shirt. The sharp sliver had gone all the way through to her back. A lot of blood was pouring from the wound. Suddenly, her back stiffened. She felt a chill crawl across her scalp as warning bells went off in her brain! *Something was there!* ***Don't look!*** the tiny voice inside her shouted…but the impulse was strong. With dread, she slowly turned her head, and *slap!* there on the opposite bank was the *thing* that had been on the ridge! The sharp impact paralyzed her. When it opened and flexed its wings, Sherry knew it wasn't a bear or a wolf. The creature had a long thin snout and bared its bat-like teeth. Twitching and flogging its tail on the ground like a whip, its black, lupine eyes bored into her. Adrenaline hit her brain like a shot. More terrified than anytime in her life, she ran, screaming, farther up the creek bank. Screeching like a banshee, the predator rose in the air. Above and to the back of her, she heard wings flapping and knew the *screak* was coming after her.

Holding her bleeding side, she clawed her way up a steep briar-choked hill. She was nearly to the top, when she heard the sound of a motor. Crashing out of the bushes onto a narrow, gravel road, she was just in time to see a logging truck, red taillights winking, go around a bend. *"Stop!"* Sherry, her strained larynx nearly a whisper, pleaded, *"Oh, please come back!"* Desperately, she ran down the desolate, tree-draped, pine-rustling lane after the disappearing vehicle.

Suddenly, out of the woods, a blood-curdling *screeeeeeeeech* and the *pflap pflap* of heavy wings were in the air. Then, with a *thud*, the thing hit the ground. She heard its feet running *thwack thwack* behind her. Leaping into the bushes beside the road, it kept pace with her.

The rain-swollen black clouds quickly brought on the darkness, as she ran blindly along the muddy road. Abruptly, she fell and expecting the demon to attack her, struggled to her feet. But, panting like a dog, it had stopped. She then realized the creature was toying with her and when it grew tired of the game, would spring on her. Nevertheless, she trotted down the forbidding, murky ribbon into an opaque void.

At the top of a rise, a full moon suddenly burst through the clouds. Something metallic was squeaking *Creak! Creak! Creak!* in the wind. Not too far ahead, she could see two round, red reflectors glowing in the dark. Nearing them, she saw a hinged sign fiercely swinging back and forth, boasting *Jason's Hide-a-way.* Recognizing the driveway to her cabin and, with a desire to live, she was able to pick up speed. When she made the turn, she heard the wilding come out of the bushes and onto the road behind her. Smelling the stench of its breath as it closed in on her, she jumped on the porch, whamming into the wall. Jerking the doorknob, she realized the door was locked. *Think, Sherry!* went through her head. *Where's the key?* Afraid to turn around—by now, her screaming was more like the grunt of a pig - she ran her hand under the windowsill and found the key. Fearing the *thing* was about to grab her, she dropped the key twice before getting it in the slot. Just before she slammed and locked the door, she saw **It!** *With tail whipping the ground, it was sitting in the driveway not twenty feet away!* Fangs glinting in the bright moonlight, the wolfish fiend grinned at her. Then, the black clouds took the moon away.

Rachel came awake. The alarm clock was screaming. Reaching to turn it off, she found she couldn't roll over. Something was holding her down and she couldn't remember where she was. It was getting dark, but she could see the tree lying across her. Feeling the bark with her hands, memory started coming back. It hadn't been the alarm clock! Someone *had* been screaming! *It was Sherry!*

"Sherry!" Rachel yelled. *"Sherrrrrrry!! Help me, Sherry! I can't move! Sherrrrrrrrrrrrrrry!"*

Overhead, she heard the flapping of heavy wings and an ear-piercing shriek. Something big was flying around up there. Sherry was screaming again. She called out to her, but the noise was moving further away. Then the wind picked up again and whispered eerily through the pines. The temperature was dropping.

Mercifully, there was no feeling below her waist. Her head hurt from the fall over the dam, and her arm throbbed from being hit by the big stick. Water pooled around her on the sandbar, cooling her scratches from the thicket. She was soaking wet and cold. The combination of gasoline fumes and yelling for Sherry had made her voice weak. The clogged-up waterfall was overhead and to the right. Hearing the water as it sloshed over the side, she hoped the clog would hold.

Where was Sherry? Rachel decided her friend was either dead or gone for help. But why had the girl been screaming? Suddenly, there was a loud crack above her and the sound of gushing water. She knew part of the dam had given way. *It won't be long,* she thought, *before the whole thing goes!*

She had sold a lot of cookies for the Girl Scouts - learned healthful, character building activities…and also, had learned to build a fire. One of the few useful things she had grasped in her irresponsible lifetime. The wind whistled around the house as Sherry sat on the floor in front of the fireplace, with Jason's shotgun across her lap. She held the shell-casing full of shot in her hand, not knowing how to open the gun barrel to load it. It was a toss-up - which hurt the worse—her bleeding side or the scratches all over her body. *It's going to come in and get me,* she thought. *I can't stop it! Why didn't I let Jason show me how to use the gun?* But the tiny voice inside her said, *Don't worry about it. Nothing can stop it, anyway.* She was getting too weak to care. Shock was settling in. She opened a bottle of Justin's pain pills his dentist had given him when he'd had oral surgery. The dose was one tablet every four hours. She swallowed two with a big swig of bourbon. Soon the loss of blood, the warmth from the fire, whiskey, and the drugs put her to sleep.

The water was trying to run into her ears. Rachel tried holding her head higher with her hand under her neck thinking, *It's only a matter of time,* and knowing she would drown before getting out. She remembered reading once, the most powerful lesson in life is the one that teaches us what we already know to be the truth. Looking back on her life and the people she loved, she mostly thought of Jeff. A career had been more important and that had ruined her marriage. The doctor warned her if she didn't slow down and rest, she would lose the baby and, of course, she hadn't listened. There was the painful memory of Jeff standing over her hospital bed and saying he was through. She relived the emptiness when she came home and he was gone. Now, he wanted a divorce. His girlfriend was pregnant. He was getting the son she lost. *If I had another chance, Jeff, I would do it differently,* and knowing she would never get that chance, she began to cry.

The Wauler was on the porch. It went over to a thick pool of blood and licked it up, absorbing all that was Sherry: her hopes, her dreams and all her memories. It leaped from the porch edge into the yard and went over and sat in the driveway. *Sherrrrry!* it called in her mother's voice, *Sherry, honey, it's Momma.*

"Momma?" Sherry croaked, coming awake. Hearing a noise at the door, and letting the shotgun slide to the floor, she struggled to her feet. Holding her bleeding side and staggering across the room, she grated out, "Momma, is that you? How did you find me?" *Yesss, Sherrry, Baaaby, it's Mommma. Open the doooor.* And, when she did that, she realized her mistake.

The water was getting deeper. It was above her shoulders. Having managed to grasp a branch on the tree, Rachel was in a nearly sitting position. The limb was just barely in reach of her good arm, and she could feel the strain on her shoulder blade. Wait! Did she feel the tree move? There! It trembled again!

The Wauler dropped Sherry in the hole it had dug - not very far from where the hunter had been buried, nearly a fortnight ago. The carrion was ripe and about ready to be dug up. The same thing would happen to Sherry's body in the same amount of days. With hind legs, the creature kicked dirt and leaves over the carcass; that done, it spread its wings and flew away.

Rachel heard it fly over in the dark and land in the bushes by the side of the creek. She thought it was probably the same varmint that had flown over earlier. Whatever it was, it was big. The wind had died down and there was an unnatural quietness in the forest. Nothing stirred. Then, *Snap! A* twig broke. Leaves rustled, and she knew it was coming. It stunk. The odor was similar to a dead skunk she'd smelled once—only this was much worse.
Rachel, Sweetheart, I've come to get you out.
She jumped at Jeff's voice. "Jeff? Is that really you?
Yesssss, my love, it's me, and I'll soon get you out.
She heard it leave the bushes, flapping its wings. With a heavy thud and scratching claws, it landed on her tree.
"Here I am, Darling!" it shrieked.
"You're not Jeff! I don't know what you are, but you're not Jeff!"
Only the keen, pointed ears of that winged, abominable beast from hell could hear her now.

Suddenly, with a sucking sound, the tree came loose from the sandbar. She heard a roar like a train coming down the mountain, and realizing it was flashflood waters, grasped the tree tighter. Then, with a thunder, the clog blew from the waterfall. In an instant, the powerful force of water shot her, the Wauler and the tree down the creek. She knew her fate was with the tree, so she literally hung on for dear life.

The clouds rolled away again, uncovering a full moon. The creature sat on hind legs in front of her, facing the direction the tree was pell-melling.

Throwing its head back, and snout pointing skyward, it howled at the moon. *AHHOOooooooooooooooo! AHHOOOooooooooooooooooooo!* There was a faraway answering wail that reverberated through the mountains.

Turning its head, the Wauler said, in The Little-Girl-Lost-And-Never-Found's sweet voice, *There's another big ol' waterfall coming up. Better brace yourself, now.* And just at the instant they reached the falls, it promised, in the Cessna pilot's deep voice, *See y'all at the bottom,* lifted its wings and flew off.

When the tree hit the outcropping rock at the top of the waterfall, Rachel was torn loose and flung out over the lake below. With her face toward the heavens, the last thing she ever saw was Venus, the evening star. Her last regrets were of things she had thought important that didn't much matter now, and the last words she was ever to whisper were, "Jeff, I'm sorry."

The Wauler, dragging carrion with a red hunter's cap still sticking to the scalp, went down into its lair. The wilding was hungry and, although pleased with full larders, excitedly anticipated its next prey. Not needing the meat in a plentiful environment, it enjoyed the hunt. After eating, the creature curled up and slept. Suddenly, dark, marble eyes shot open. The silence of the wildwood was broken. *Momma is that you?* Sherry's voice asked, then Rachel's answered, *Jeff, I'm sorry.* In anticipation, the varmint sat up on its haunches. The hunter's deep bass voice told the piles of gnawed bones, *There's a stalking moon tonight and humans are in the forest!*

Now I Lay Me Down to Sleep
by
Glenda Mills

Then
There were monsters
Lying in wait under my bed
Lurking in my closet
Leering with glowing eyes
Through my windows
Horrible creatures of imagination
My mantra of reassurance
Monsters don't exist

Now
There are images
Bodies broken by violence
Battlefields of horror
Banished forgotten souls
Tormented by
Hatred, prejudice, misunderstanding
My mantra of reality
Monsters do exist

The Moving Mansion
by
Joanna Foreman

Athens, Alabama—1953. Elmer Joseph Boonswallow's death occurred early on a frosty, January morning. In his colossal suite on the third floor of Boonswallow Manor, his antique English canopy bed was encircled by a doctor, three nursemaids in crisp, white uniforms, and a horde of family members. Freshly pressed handkerchiefs dabbed eyes, sobs and moans echoed down the corridor and around the corner into the adjacent sector of the stately mansion.

If the house servants had been tucked into their assigned spaces, they would have easily heard the commotion from their quarters, one floor below. But they were attentive, on-call at the entrance area of their master's domain, tending to the family's many needs—*a shawl for my wife, quickly now! Earl Grey with lemon (and make it hotter than the last pot); an upholstered chair (this one is much too uncomfortable); tend that fire (Boy, can't you feel the chill in this room?).* On and on they whined.

Elmer Joseph, AKA Elmo Joe, was not surrounded by loved ones because he, himself, was a loved man. Not by a long shot.

Where there's a will, there's family, and Elmo Joe's Last Will & Testament, concealed in a locked box, was to be read within minutes of his death by his legal representative. The lawyer, Wilbur Mayberry, was a wiry fellow with gray whiskers and a handlebar mustache. He hovered in one corner of the room, fidgeting with a key in the left pocket of his pinstripe pants.

Elmo Joe lived to the age of 103. He had lingered during the last two years, precariously teetering on the edge. His death had taken way too long; the final family scene had been reenacted four times already. His great-nephews wondered if he would ever die at all.

Everyone muttered and sniveled with relief. The moment they had waited for had arrived. Each person in the room expected to get a piece of Elmo Joe. And why shouldn't they? He had enough pieces to go around two or three times. They would all be rich and—the very best part—rid of Elmo Joe forever. That's what they thought.

◆━━━━━━━◆━━━━━━━◆

Elmo Joe was born in 1850 to wealthy parents. Twenty years later they surprised him with a baby sister. (His parents were considerably stunned, as well.) He called her Sister.

Through the years, Porter, his brother-in-law, had squandered Sister's inheritance, which was not surprising to Elmo Joe. He had always suspected the man to be more interested in Sister's financial value than her happiness. What little savings Porter and Sister had left vanished on Black Tuesday, October 29, 1929.

Elmo Joe had invested his share of the family money wisely and prospered during even the worst of the Great Depression in 1933, shaking his head at the young whippersnappers who didn't. He loaned Porter and Sister money to help them get back on their feet, but at an exorbitant rate of interest. They, in turn, loaned some of the money to their own children and grandchildren at a higher percentage, which allowed them to make their own timely payments. *Timely payments, timely payments*—notorious phrasing in all of Elmo Joe's business contracts.

Elmo Joe owned two high-rise apartment buildings in Huntsville, and though he wasn't a slumlord, he was known for being slow in the maintenance department. On occasion, the elevator would not work (not a good thing for the elderly living on the higher floors), and he switched over to a boiler heating system the first day of September, eliminating the ability to use air-conditioning, even though temperatures in early fall were routinely over seventy-five degrees.

He was a demanding landlord and insisted his tenants follow his distinct Rules of Apartment Living—or else. He would not allow the walls to be painted any color other than white; this applied also to ceilings, of course. He allowed no frying of fish (it stunk up the entire building), no smoking indoors, no loud music, and definitely no pets of any kind, not even an old lady's yellow canary. Upon routine inspection, he had found one in a widow's studio unit on the fifteenth floor and immediately evicted her (after he opened the cage door, dispatching the bird out the open window—never to be seen again).

Elmo Joe rented to his nephews and nieces at a discount—five percent—but only if they paid one month in advance. If their payment was overdue, he demanded the cumulative discount he had allowed them for the entire period of their past lease. If they were unable to come up with the money in seven days, he moved them out in spite of their pleadings—set them right out on the sidewalk—like any other negligent tenant.

One day, Elmo Joe had wondered if God felt the same satisfaction as he did when He was called upon to punish irresponsible people. But he was a non-religious man, and later that same day he remembered that he had previously come to the educated conclusion that God does not exist.

When Elmo Joe pulled their strings, both family and business acquaintances danced like marionettes. They endured his eccentricities and jumped through his nonsensical hoops for the financial advantages it provided them.

Wilbur Mayberry read the will aloud in the library. Everyone in the audience sat straight in their chairs, eager with anticipation.

The estate's assets were listed as follows:

> Two luxury high-rise buildings
> An innumerable amount of stocks and
> bearer bonds worth millions
> A Savings and Loan office in Florence
> A prosperous Ford dealership in Decatur
> Half-ownership in a new steak and pan-
> cake enterprise (whose franchises were
> selling like…well, hotcakes).

Porter and Sister, now in their early eighties, delightedly added numbers in their heads. They figured they would inherit the most. They would travel the world—first class, of course.

Only those present in the room at Elmo Joe's death were to be beneficiaries. Anyone else was out in the cold. (Mayberry's secretary had leaked that fact as rumor, which explains why the bedroom suite had been filled to capacity that day.)

Other than the mansion, all assets were to be sold and placed in a fund, aptly called Boonswallow Manor Trust, to provide for maintenance and repair.

The heirs—the doctor, nurses, lawyer, family members and servants alike—shared the benefits of Boonswallow Manor Trust equally. But there was a catch: To claim the inheritance, they all had to live together in the mansion. The trust would generate a hefty monthly allowance for each family member unless they chose to move out of the house.

Elmo Joe's Rules of Apartment Living applied here, too. The walls could not be painted any color but white, no fish frying, no smoking, no loud music, no pets, and so forth.

Once the initial shock wore off, cries and moans of horror emanated throughout the manor.

The great-nephews and nieces tried to comfort their parents and grandparents. They pointed out that they had lived by these rules previously—these conditions were nothing new—but the older crowd was inconsolable. Their agitation was caused by the fact that they had to share their windfall with the lawyer, the doctor, the nurses and the servants, each of whom was to receive a generous annual stipend.

Wilber Mayberry curiously watched the pandemonium. He recalled Elmo Joe's obnoxious laugh the day he signed his will. *How disgusting that he can control people from the grave,* he thought. Mayberry had moved into the mansion two weeks ago and planned to remain, although it troubled him to think he would have to live in the close vicinity of the others. He looked forward to semi-retirement, and he planned to pursue his favorite pastime—fishing in Wheeler Lake near Muscle Shoals. He knew he couldn't fry fish in the house, but grilling them on his campsite would suffice, a small price to pay for the luxuries he was about to enjoy. He couldn't believe his luck and was one of the few present who actually appreciated what Elmo Joe had given him.

Mayberry patiently waited for the bedlam to calm down before he read the final request of Elmer Joseph Boonswallow:

> *My corpse shall be embalmed, interred in a customized gold coffin, sealed in a vault that has been constructed in the cellar of Boonswallow Manor.*
>
> *The Manor will never be sold or demolished. If it is sold or demolished, said estate recipients will forfeit all future*

> *inheritance. In that instance, the remain-*
> *ing funds in Boonswallow Manor Trust*
> *will be distributed to the United States*
> *Government to use as it sees fit.*

All twenty-six bedrooms of the manor were occupied by the heirs, and eventually most of them learned to get along. Some quickly found the Rules of Apartment Living tedious, however.

Sister grew tired of her bedroom's white walls, for she was a colorful woman who had always preferred jewel-toned decorating. She hired a painter; the east wall he painted sunshine yellow, the west wall royal purple, the north wall brilliant red, and the south wall jungle green. Sister was delighted with the results and tipped him generously.

The next morning when she awakened she opened her eyes and shrieked in terror. Her great-grandchildren ran down the hall and into her room to see what her problem might be.

All the walls were white, as though they had never been painted! Sister demanded her money back from the painter, but he refused.

One of the nurses had a Siamese cat and was determined to move it into the mansion with her. She kept it secreted away, but soon it went missing. She looked in every nook and cranny, anywhere a cat might find a hiding place, but the feline was never found.

The doctor had kept his smoking habit a secret from everyone. He felt it was a shame that a man who took care of others' health would do something so careless to his own. The day he moved in, he un-packed three cartons of Winston cigarettes and hid them in a drawer with a secret bottom. The next morning, he slid the bottom of the drawer open, only to find it empty.

Wilber Mayberry was the last one to deviate. He had taken a long-awaited fishing trip to Oregon, and he returned with a large catch of salmon. He spent one afternoon in the sizeable kitchen, prepared various vegetable side dishes, rubbed an herbal mixture on the salmon and baked it in the commercial-style wall oven. He was joined in the dining room that evening by the other household members who con-sumed the gourmet feast with delight.

The next morning, the kitchen was locked, the deadbolt shut from inside. Seven days later, remarkably, the lock came open, just as curiously as it had been bolted the week before. They had apparently suffered a loss of power in the kitchen. Servants tossed out bags of spoiled food and completely cleaned and sanitized the refrigerator.

"Great-uncle Elmo's ghost inhabits this house," voiced a relative. "The Rules have been ignored!"

"But the salmon was baked, not fried," the doctor said.

"The odor is still a fishy one," a servant added.

"Perhaps it's simply better not to toy with the Rules," said the doctor.

The heirs held a household meeting and decided to strictly abide by the Rules of Apartment Living rather than create any further madness. For the next eight years, no one ever ventured down to the cellar, for the one thing they all agreed upon was that Elmo Joe's ghost definitely inhabited it.

Then, something entirely unexpected happened. The Highway Department was bringing Interstate 65 through, purchasing land, tearing down houses. The plans called for the freeway to cut right through the middle of Boonswallow Manor.

Mayberry battled with a number of stubborn officials to get them to understand fully the complexity of the situation. The Last Will and Testament had specifically stated the manor could not be demolished for any reason. Everyone would move, lose their liberal monthly incomes, and worse yet—the remaining millions of dollars held in trust would be handed over to the United States Government. That outlook was particularly distasteful to residents, but the officials insisted they had to get the structure out of highway's path, one way or another.

Which gave Mayberry an idea—*move* Boonswallow Manor!

It took a serious amount of palm-greasing for the Highway Department to reach an agreement with the estate recipients. The house would be transported nine-hundred feet to the west and settled on a fine, six-acre section of prime land.

The lawyer called a household meeting. The heirs had only one question. What about the cellar?

"It will be filled in immediately upon the removal of the manor," Mayberry explained. "The Highway Department offered to pour a new cellar if we so desire."

Wide-eyed, everyone's thoughts went downward to Elmo Joe's

solid gold coffin, and, without another word, they boarded up the walls of the cellar, hiding any evidence of the vault's presence below.

The manor was moved without incident—the cellar filled with concrete.

Boonswallow Manor has changed for the better.

Sister spends summers traveling throughout Europe with her granddaughters. When in Alabama, she enjoys vibrant, colorful walls in her boudoir.

The doctor bought a burgundy, silk smoking-jacket and rolls his own smokes with a custom blend of tobacco.

Rock and roll forcefully echoes from the rooms of the youth.

The cat-loving nurse has Butters, a female Siamese, and a lady Persian named Picnic. She is considering an Abyssinian male which she will call Encore.

Wilber Mayberry is an avid angler at Wheeler Lake. He fries trout and smallmouth bass in the manor's kitchen, and complements his meals with a variety of the other residents' favorites: cheese grits, fried apples, hush-puppies, sliced tomatoes, fried okra and iced tea. The entire household joins him in the stately dining room every Monday night. They occasionally package up their leftovers for donation to a homeless shelter in Huntsville.

Trucks and automobiles on Interstate-65 unknowingly drive right over a solid gold coffin, eight feet below, but Elmo Joe's ghost is trapped inside and there is not one thing he can do about it.

We hope.

The Moving Mansion was originally printed in the book: Ghosts of Interstate-65, Quixote Press © 2008 by Joanna Foreman

Contributors

The Southern Indiana Writers Group has been more-or-less together since 1992. We began meeting monthly in a conference room in a local hospital. We now meet weekly to exchange information and expertise on everything from computers to poetry. The group also serves as a critique forum (in the same sense that a pack of wolves serves as food critics). Membership is limited, but visitors are welcome, and have been known to fit in so well they become members against their better judgment.

Bonnie Abraham After twenty-five plus years of writing letters disqualifying people from Unemployment Benefits, she retired in order to write something more pleasant. She writes short stories (many with Biblical themes), poetry and devotionals. Currently, she resides in Corydon with her mother's ghost.

Marian Allen lives in a big house in a little wood, which is not the only difference between Allen and Laura Ingels Wilder. She has published stories in print and on-line magazines, including Marion Zimmer Bradley's FANTASY Magazine, The Phone Book, PanGaia and Oceans of the Mind.

Jeannine Baumgartle writes poetry and fiction. Her work has appeared in publications such as *Green Meadow Press*, *Flying Island, Literally*, and Studio: *A Journal for Christians Writing* and won a residency for poetry at the Mary Anderson Center for the Arts . She and her husband live in the small town of Crandall.

Ginny Fleming considers herself to be foremost a screenwriter, as this is her favorite media. Her romantic comedy scripts can be previewed at The Spec Script Library, Writer's Market, and Writers.Net. Besides her annual contribution to SIWG anthology, and a brief appearance in the Louisville Courier Journal, Fleming's next project is finding a home for Keys of Illusion, a Romantic/Suspense novel filled with magic, scuba, fantasy, a bunch of lavender stuff and little bit of sex.

Joanna Foreman writes short fiction and slice-of-life vignettes. Her first collection of short stories, *Ghosts of Interstate 65,* was published in January, 2008. She is currently working on her first novel which is set along the River Walk in San Antonio, Texas. Her frequent weekend getaways to the River Walk keep her in touch with the imaginary characters living there. Above all, Joanna's first priority is family, although she occasionally experiences sudden urges to move to the moon for escape purposes. Her ten-year-old granddaughter advises her to take her cell phone so she can be kept abreast of the family's shenanigans while she is gone. Joanna and her husband Craig married barefooted on St. Augustine Beach in 2001. They built a modest home smack-dab in the middle of two wooded acres and will live happily ever after.

Mary Gehant-Lagunez was born in Duluth, Minnesota, and has lived most of her life in Louisville, Kentucky. She is a graduate (French Literature) of Carleton College, Northfield, Minnesota. She now calls New Albany, Indiana, home, and has a second home in Cuernavaca, Mexico. She worked in the promotion department of WHAS, Inc. The last assignment she had was as promotion writer, handling publicity for all three stations and the stations' chief public service program, the WHAS Crusade for Children. Gehant-Lagunez then served in the Public Information Department for the Commonwealth of Kentucky. She is married to Dr. Mario Lagunez, who is retired from the faculty of Purdue University. She is currently editing a book for George M. Wolverton, M.D.

Dirk Griffin, also known as The Invisible Man. Dirk is seldom among us in reality, but reality has never been our strong suit, anyway. He has written theatre reviews for Arts Kentuckiana, had a script produced for Public Access Television, and has written music/lyrics and/or scripts for several musicals. Bunbury Theatre of Louisville, Kentucky, selected one of Griffin's plays to include in their 2001 15th Anniversary 15 Minute Play Festival.

Elizabeth J. Gross (nee Norwood) Since the drought of '99, she no longer gets her living from the river. She lives in a big house with no woods. While she has won a few awards for her poetry, she has also received citations to get out of town. Her only fears: tar and feathers.

T Lee Harris is a writer and illustrator who has been a lover of mystery and the detective genre since discovering books. A graduate of Indiana University with a Bachelor of Fine Arts, T has been involved with radio production, game design, comic books and desktop publishing. Interests include participation in the Society for Creative Anachronism and Renaissance Faires, tailoring authentic costuming for re-enactors and playing online roleplaying games. Several novels are in progress featuring Sitehuti and Nefer-Djenou-Bastet, Josh Katzen and a series set in ninth century Ireland. Work has appeared in print and online venues including mystericale.com and Cat Tales.

Joy Kirchgessner lives in Corydon with her husband, Mike. Her interests are too vast to list on this page. She's a long time business woman of Corydon, and artist, whose nature paintings have been accepted into prestigious shows, photographer, whose photographs have joined her illustrations in our anthologies, equestrian, who enjoys trail rides, amateur archaeologist, who enjoys rock hunting and exploring new worlds—give her a chemistry set and a laboratory and she'd try to split atoms. Many years ago, Southern Indiana Writers tied her to a computer and wonderful stories blossomed from Kirchgessner's many interests. So now, she must add accomplished writer to that long, long list. She even has a novel or two in the early stages.

George Lopez is a practicing architect, a construction specifications writer, and figurative sculptor. His profession obliges him to travel extensively, exposing him to a diversity of people and circumstances. George draws upon these experiences for his fiction writing. He is currently marketing several short stories, and is working on a novel, which he shares with the group as it progresses.

Glenda Mills resides in New Albany, Indiana with her husband and youngest son. She has a daughter and a son who no longer live at home and one grandchild. When she is not busy homemaking, homeschooling, attending soccer games, running the family taxi service, or volunteering at her church, she writes fiction, nonfiction, and poetry. She looks forward to the day when a person can actually be in two places at once.

Previous Publications by
Southern Indiana Writers

Indian Creek Anthology
Ghost Writers
Christmas Bizarre
Dragon: Our Tales
Grounds for Suspicion
2000 Tales
Way Out West
Unbridled Lust
There's Something Under the Bedtime Stories
Novel Ingredients
Write of Passage
Off the Rack
Beastly Tales
It's Always Something
Most Wanted

Coming Soon:

FUTURE
PERFECT
(TENSE IN SPACE)

Visit our web site for excerpts of previous publications
and availability information:

http://southernindianawriters.com